An

VINCENT BANVILLE is a writer, critic and journalist living in Dublin. His first novel, *An End to Flight*, won the Robert Pitman Literary Prize. He is also the author of five children's books, the *Hennessy* series, along with three crime novels, *Death by Design*, *Death the Pale Rider* and *Cannon Law*. He is *The Irish Times* crime critic.

AN END TO FLIGHT

Vincent Banville

NEW ISLAND

AN END TO FLIGHT
First published 1973 by Faber and Faber Limited
This edition published November 2002 by New Island
2 Brookside, Dundrum Road, Dublin 14

ISBN 1 904301 00 2

British Library Cataloguing in Publication Data.
A CIP catalogue record for this book is available
from the British Library.

Typeset by New Island
Cover design by Artmark
Cover Image: Getty Images
Printed by Cox & Wyman, Reading, Berks.

The Arts Council
An Chomhairle Ealaíon

New Island receives financial assistance from The Arts Council,
(An Chomhairle Ealaíon), Dublin, Ireland.

To David Marcus

Biafra's aims in this war cannot justify even one death. But what is the alternative? You stand still, you get killed. You run away, and you will be killed. In the northernmost parts of Nigeria, they started slaughtering our people. We kept running, running, running. Having crossed a line, we called it home. This is what Biafra is, an end to a journey and an end to flight.

General Chukwuemeka Odumegwu Ojukwu

Part One

LAST SUPPER

1

Painter put his hand on the table and then took it away and looked at the sticky imprint it left behind on the dusty surface. He put his hand back again, carefully settling each finger down exactly on its corresponding impression. He leaned hard on the heel of his hand so that the knuckles tightened and his fingers curled up under the pressure. Sweat stood out on his forehead, stayed for a moment in greasy blobs, became drops, and rolled down the sides of his face and plopped softly onto his bare shoulders. He leaned back in his chair.

The room he was sitting in was completely anonymous; it had no distinguishing features whatever. The furniture, a table, some hard chairs, four padded easy chairs in aseptic plastic covers, a water filter standing in the corner, the torn faded curtains, they were objects which fulfilled a purpose and that was all. A few personal possessions were scattered about, a guitar with two broken strings, some books on the small round table inside the door, a calendar advertising Star beer, but none of these impinged on the general colourlessness.

Painter stood up. He was wearing only a pair of dirty khaki shorts and he needed a shave. He padded across the floor in his bare feet, under the archway and through the open back door. There was a strip of concrete yard behind the house stretching out to about six feet, then a half-hearted attempt at a garden, and finally a row of stable-like one-roomed houses running parallel to the main building.

It was raining, steady monotonous rain falling effortlessly from a grey sky. Over the door, where Painter was standing, the chute was damaged and a snake of water fell straight down and spattered on the cement. Painter stood under this and looked across at his cook's house. The door was closed and the house seemed deserted, but he knew that the boy was inside. He was entertaining his woman; it was a proper activity for such an evening but it irritated Painter to think that the boy had company, while he was alone.

He shouted, "Jude," and then louder, "Jude, I want you."

The door opened slowly, as if mirroring the boy's unwillingness, as he came out and moved across the ground towards Painter. Jude was about seventeen, with a smooth brown face and body, and he walked on his toes, as if he had forgotten to put on his shoes. He stopped before the cement step and stood in the rain, looking up at Painter. Painter stepped out from under the deluge. His flesh was white, with a slight bluish tinge, and the water had plastered his hair down on his head like a skullcap. He shivered in the cold air.

"I forgot what I wanted you for," he said. He looked around him vaguely and then back at the boy, who had not moved. There were no sounds, only the rain fell between them like a soft swishing curtain, and out behind the few decrepit palm trees lightning flickered intermittently.

Painter rocked back on his heels and leaned against the wall. "Have you a woman in your house?" he said.

The boy hesitated for a moment, then he said, "Woman, she be there."

"What do you talk about when she visits you?" Painter said. He wrapped his arms about his body and, when the boy did not answer, he walked the length of the concrete strip. When he came back he stood in front of the boy again and asked him, "Do you tell her that she's beautiful? That you want to be with her every minute of every hour of every day?"

10

Jude shrugged. He seemed to have no interest in the conversation. He said, "She be good for fuck."

"And tomorrow?"

"Tomorrow she go Owerri side, my money not be there anymore."

"Is that all? Is it only a business transaction? Is she merely a whore?"

"She be good girl, only sixteen years old. You want her?"

The boy spoke dispassionately, as if he were talking about a piece of discarded furniture or a worn-out garment.

Painter looked at the sky and closed his eyes against the persistent rain. The firmament was blue up behind those clouds, and from up above, under the sun, the clouds probably resembled great billowing rolls of candy floss. He thought of some lines of poetry he had learned a long time ago:

God's in his heaven,
All's right with the world.

It did not seem to follow, not today.

"You want her?" the boy said again. "She no speak English good. She be Rivers people, from Calabar."

"Aha," Painter said, "uncut toto."

"You say?"

"She's not circumcised, like your Ibo women."

"What difference, there be room to go in and come out." The boy grinned, but it took Painter a moment to realise that he had made a joke.

Away in the west the sun suddenly appeared for a moment, peering out under the frayed hem of the clouds like a proprietary master checking to see if his subjects were behaving themselves. But the clouds soon closed in again and thunder rolled like the lowering of a giant portcullis.

Painter squeezed his eyes tightly shut and then opened them again, but shiny black dots still swarm at the edge of his vision like frogspawn seen through water. He went back

11

inside the house and closed the door. Then he opened it again. The boy had not moved and Painter waved an arm aimlessly at him.

Inside the house it was beginning to get dark, although it was only five o'clock. The crickets must have been fooled by the early darkness, for they had already begun their nightly crepitation. A breeze like a sharp intake of breath stirred the curtains and the rain began to fall harder, drumming on the corrugated iron roof and splashing through the louvred windows onto the stone floor.

Painter stood in the middle of the room, water dropping off him and soaking into the matting which covered the centre of the floor. He thought again of his vision of the sun above the clouds, and now a jetplane, small and silvery like a child's toy, silently glided across the cumulus of cloudbank. It had been like that when he was coming out to Nigeria, lifting off from a misty, fog-enshrouded London after the short trip from Dublin, beating through the wreaths of grey spume, until suddenly the harsh glare of the sun took him by surprise and caused him to look out upon a marshmallow world of space and silence. The old man beside him had stretched his head sideways out of his cocoon of clothes like a snail arching out of its shell, away from the sun and the vivid blue of the sky. It had been Painter's first flight and he had badly wanted to talk to someone, but his withered seatmate had only spoken once during the trip, and that was to ask the hostess to pull the shade across the window. He had sat behind his sunglasses all the way to Kano; he did not read, or write, or do anything in particular. He had been as old and still and silent as a leaf fallen from a tree in autumn.

Painter shivered again. His hands were so cold that he had difficulty in lighting the Aladdin lamp, and when he did get it going, it burned unevenly and cast paroxysms of shadows about the walls. And when the girl appeared in the doorway and moved into the room, until she was standing just inside the circle of light, it was as if one of the shadows had detached itself and had come alive.

Painter stood, still bent over, with the burned match in his hand, and looked at her. She was small and slight and she looked achingly vulnerable, and the rain glistened in the whorls of her short crispy hair like frost on a Christmas tree. Painter felt a sudden urge to weep; he actually felt the sting of tears in his eyes, and a sound, not unlike a sob, welled out of his throat and hung in the silence of the room. He put out his arms and the girl moved forward until she was standing close against him and he could feel her warmth seeping into his own cold body. She exuded a faint perfume like sandalwood and when he put his hands on her shoulders, the wraparound she was wearing opened over the soft smoothness of her back. She put her face in the hollow of his shoulder and he could feel her lips fluttering against his flesh like the wings of some small trapped bird.

Still holding her with one hand, he picked up the lamp and they went into the bedroom. When they lay on the bed he entered her almost at once, but then he stopped moving and closed his eyes. The girl worked her pelvis, but when Painter did not respond she too became motionless, her head still in the hollow of his neck and her eyes, wide open, gazing across him at the darkened window.

Painter moaned, not loudly, but pleasurably. A gecko lizard on the lamplit wall, as perfect and fragile as a fern leaf, moved fractionally closer to the large powdery moth it was stalking. Painter felt himself stir inside the girl, the faintest tremor, and his whole body began to relax towards the focal point of his member in its fleshy sheath. The moth fluttered its wings and the gecko lizard froze within inches of its prey. As the rain sifted softly in through the open window, the lamplight waned and the lizard darted forward again. The girl moved her head and looked into Painter's

13

face, but his eyes were blank and unfocused like the eyes of a drowned man. Only his organ was tremendous inside her and she shuddered on it, feeling it grow, making it fill her until she dissolved about it in strength and pain and a cry; and the gecko lizard made its final assault, snapping up the frantic moth and disappearing with it under the flat roof.

2

When Painter awoke the girl was gone. The sheets on the bed were cold and clammy and the lamp was beginning to smoke. A piece of cord, stretching from the handle of the wardrobe to the wire frame over the window, supported a line of clothes on wooden hangers, and in one corner of the room a camp bed sagged forlornly.

He went across to the window and looked out at the rain which was falling straight down, hard and long, beating down the leaves on the tattered palm trees, spiking little wet disappearing holes in the brown clay and sliding darkly across the stone pathway leading up to the house. The nightwatch went by; a dark featureless figure carrying a lantern like an ancient town crier but tolling no reassuring sounds for his unseen listeners. Painter crooked the fingers of both his hands around the wire mesh and leaned his forehead against its coolness. If the rain would only stop. If a wind tasting of the sea would only blow to stir the drooping folds of the mosquito net. I would catch that wind, he thought. I'd trap it deep down in my lungs, in the pores of my body, and I'd guard it jealously like a memory of childhood. He stood on his toes as if he were trying to see over the top of a high wall, but outside the arc of lamplit stone verandah and brown clay the darkness was impenetrable, and if sea winds bloomed they did so for someone else in some other place.

He was still standing in the same position when the school generator rumbled and the lights sprang on all over

15

the house. Jude came in quietly and began to dress the bed, his movements slow and deliberate, and the muscles rippling under the flesh of his bare shoulders.

Painter turned from the window. "Why did you send the girl to me?" he asked the boy.

"She came herself, I no send her."

"Will she come again?"

"No, she gone Owerri side. More business be there."

"Carrying my seed."

"You say?"

"Never mind."

Painter put on clean underwear and clean socks. He ran a hand over the stubble on his face but then shrugged and finished dressing. It was his fourth Wet Season in Nigeria and he had woken up that morning to find the first traces of fungus in his groin. This had happened to him in his first Wet Season also, when his scrotum had turned into something that resembled green cheese. The ubiquitous mould attacked everything, clothes in the darkness of a wardrobe, cameras unprotected by silica gel, food, table joints, chairs, curtains, and even Painter's own most private parts. It was insidious, it stank like the odour of wet clothes in a warm room and it only disappeared with the return of the sun. He had not minded too much the first time for he was young and healthy and engrossed in his work. The Ibo boys that he taught, in this privately owned school deep in the bush and thirty miles from Owerri, were so eager to learn, were so ready to absorb the facts and figures and snatches of comment that he tossed about so negligently, that he was able to ignore those little realities that refused to bolster up his idealism. Poor examination results and the increasing tedium of the narrow syllabus had, after the first year, brought a relaxing of his concentration, so that when the first storms of March had roiled the skies overhead, he had locked his door and stayed in bed, where he ate stale

16

crackers and drank innumerable bottles of Star beer, and watched the hornets build their hard mud houses in the corners of his bedroom. Then one morning he had got up, had shaved and washed, and had gone into class as usual, but the interest was not there anymore. Now it was merely a job, something to occupy the hours between eight and one, an exercise to prevent the mind from succumbing to the green deliquescent fungus.

He came out of the bedroom and went into the kitchen, where he opened the door of the fridge and took out a bottle of beer. He uncapped it and drank deeply from the bottle. Then, holding the bottle in his left hand, he went and stood at the open front door. The school was built on the side of a hill and from where he stood Painter could look down on the misty lights of the main school block and the other buildings radiating out from it down the slope of the hill towards the road. These were the houses of the African tutors, long flat functional sheds like railway carriages. Igor, the proprietor of the school, put them up and knocked them down as it suited him; they were embryonic reminders of his unwillingness to build anything durable, anything that would outlast his own lifetime.

Painter watched a light bob along the road and then turn and head in the direction of his house. The rain was still falling, but softly now, as if it could not quite make up its mind. The light came closer, skirted Painter's blue Volkswagen, and became a torch held by a young negro in a white-plastic raincoat.

"You're late, Nzendi," Painter said. He lifted the bottle and drank from it again.

"The rain ..." Nzendi said. He turned and looked back at it as if for confirmation. "I thought you would call for me."

Painter still stood blocking the doorway and the negro stood in front of him, water dripping from his plastic coat

17

and soaking into the legs of his trousers. "When did he come back?" Painter asked him. "Why didn't he contact me before this?"

Nzendi switched off his torch. He grinned suddenly and brilliantly and said, "He be back now this three days. He came on the twenty-seventh, in the morning."

"What has he been doing?"

"He sits and drinks. He does not talk very much, only about people he knew and who have gone from this place. Yesterday he went out on the lake in the rain." Nzendi shrugged and cleared his throat. He was almost a head shorter than Painter and the white powder that he had put on his face to cover his spots had caked under his eyes and at the corners of his nose, giving his features an odd unfinished look, as if he had been interrupted while removing make-up.

"I'm not well," Painter said. He stepped back into the room, under the light. The stubble stood out on his face and there were black smudges like finger marks under his eyes. "I don't think I'll go."

"He be waiting."

"Why doesn't he come and see me? I'm always here, I don't go anywhere." Painter sat down in one of the easy chairs and placed the beer bottle carefully on the floor. He put his hands under his armpits and began to shiver violently. Sweat stood out on his face, cold sweat like drops of water, and his lips drew back from his clenched teeth in a rictus of distress. Nzendi stepped inside the room and stood looking at him. After a time he relaxed, as the bout of fever passed, and he got up and wiped his face with a towel. He picked up a packet of Gold Leaf cigarettes and lit one. The whine of the generator died to a low rumble and the light waned. Painter smiled at Nzendi, who again shrugged his shoulders and grinned back at him.

Outside, the seats of the car were cold and damp to the

18

touch and the engine had to be coaxed into life. As they backed out of the driveway the headlights cut through the rain and the darkness and slid across the face of Kappel's house. It was closed against the night, still and shuttered like a summer house one sometimes sees in winter on a hill beside the sea.

The car slushed through the mud, the water spraying against the lights so that the glow from them was dim and splotched. They went down the hill and across the narrow bridge that Igor was always promising to have repaired. The town was huddled under the rain, the houses loomed up as shapeless masses and out beyond their blurred periphery, lightning poked wicked fingers into the lake. As they drew up in front of the Welfare Hotel the rain began to come down harder and one of the boys came running out to them with an umbrella.

Painter stood on the verandah for a moment and lit a cigarette. The whitewashed wall beside the doorway was stained brown with old urine and its chlorine-like smell permeated the dank hallway. The hotel was a large nondescript stone building with an enclosed courtyard and an open stairway leading to the second floor. Many of the flagstones in the courtyard were broken and large pools of water glinted dimly in the dull glow of light from the rooms which overlooked the courtyard on all four sides. Adolphus, the owner, came out of a room facing the top of the stairs. He was a small mean middle-aged African with a face like a squirrel's chewing nuts. Painter brushed past him and walked along the balcony. A woman looked furtively out of a doorway and whispered something in Ibo at him as he passed. A drum was being beaten somewhere close at hand; a soft throbbing like a half remembered headache.

Painter pushed aside a curtain and entered a room with a small bar in the corner. There were a number of chairs and red formica topped tables scattered about, and a large gaudy portrait of Queen Elizabeth hung on one wall. Ben Nzekwe stood with his back against the bar smoking a cigarette and the smoke curled like a halo about his head and hung lifelessly in the still air.

"Hello, Ben," Painter said.

Nzekwe nodded and turned to look at him. Painter tapped on the bar and shouted, "Martine." A boy of about fifteen appeared. He was a small and very black and he had a round sad face with heavy eyes. "Bring beer," Painter said.

"The town is almost deserted," Nzekwe said. "I walked about this afternoon in the rain. The houses are shuttered, the people have gone. Even Ensor's beer parlour, where the old men used to sit, it was empty. I thought they would be the last to leave."

"They believe the soldiers will be here soon," Painter said. "Their relatives came from the North and told them what it was like. They've gone for bush."

The boy came back with two bottles of beer and another glass. He came silently, under the disapproving gaze of the Queen, and poured two glasses of beer so carefully that there was no head on either of them. He went away as quietly as he had come.

"Towns are dangerous," Painter said. "Buildings, good roads, the smoke from a thousand fires, they're lucky they have the bush to go back to."

Nzekwe sighed. "Ojukwu is mad," he said. "Just like the Nigerians say he is. It would have been better to have compromised, a little is preferable to nothing."

"You say Ojukwu is mad, yet you refer to the Nigerians as if they were foreigners."

"That's what propaganda can do. Since I have come back all I have seen and heard is how we are now Biafrans, not Ibos or Nigerians, but Biafrans."

"Yes?"

"A new national identity has grown up overnight;

20

tomorrow morning I will be officially a citizen of a new republic. It's a rebirth, yet I won't feel any better than I do now. We should line up to be branded, or at least be allowed to choose."

"Christ," Painter said, "I've been sick for a week now. When I heard that you were back I thought I'd come and welcome you, but I was too sick. I can't see you properly, Ben, or hear you. Do you remember the time in Dublin when I had that monumental hangover? Everything was grey, food tasted like ashes. You visited me and brought me for a walk along by the Grand Canal. It must have been in the summer, for the water was very low, and I tried to get you to see what I could see, the pale ghost shimmering of the bodies of dead children wedged against the locks. You laughed at me and then got mad because I wouldn't fight my sickness."

"Some sicknesses you cannot fight."

"That was my line, Ben."

"And now it's mine."

Painter looked at him until he turned his head away and began to light another cigarette. "Who cares?" Painter said. He took up one of the glasses of beer and grimaced as he drank from it. "Ben, how are you? We haven't met for a year and we don't even look at one another to see if we have changed. How does England compare with Ireland? Does UCD pale to insignificance beside the splendour of Oxford? Was London free, wide and open?"

Nzekwe grinned wryly. He was a large shabby man whose thirty years rested heavily on him. He had grown a beard since Painter had last seen him and it was thick and black and covered most of his face. When Painter had met him first in Dublin he had found him frightening in the intensity of his positiveness. He had an indefinable air of self-sufficiency which the narrow parochialism of life in an Irish university did nothing to dent. The crassness and well-meant boorishness of his fellow students, the small insults

21

and unintentional indignities occasioned by the colour of his skin, rolled gently over him like idle waves. He was an intelligent, sensitive blackman who talked and drank a lot, and at the beginning Painter had taken without giving just like the rest. It was only later that he realised the extent of Ben's solitude and the anguish that tormented his soul, and by then it was almost too late. Nzekwe had left Ireland on a March day in 1962, when the wind in the trees had a sharp bite to it, and the streets of Dublin, and the faces of the people who walked those streets, were cold and withdrawn; and the airport was a cheerless bustle of impersonal activity where goodbye was merely a word caught up and lost among many; and Painter's forlorn wave as the plane taxied along the runway was as well meant, and as useless, as a slap to a child.

"The English were too polite," Nzekwe said. He went and sat down in one of the hard iron chairs. "They took me into their homes and into their hearts, but they never looked me directly in the eye. I tried to commit suicide while I was there."

"I didn't think anyone tried to commit suicide anymore."

Nzekwe went on as if he had not heard – "I sat in the bath and cut a slit in my belly, from hip to hip. The blood didn't spurt, it merely slid quietly into the bottom of the bath and there was no pain. All I could think of was the mess I was making, and of how difficult it would be for my landlady to clean up after me. I don't know how long I sat there, but I eventually got up and stood at the window until someone noticed me. Everyone was very kind and when I came out of the hospital no one mentioned it again. It was as if it had not happened."

Nzendi came into the room and stood waiting to be asked over. Painter looked at him absently and then called him over and asked him to get more beer. Outside thunder still rumbled disconsolately and a small breeze began to play about the edges of the room like a tired puppy.

Painter looked at his watch. It was twenty minutes to midnight. He said, "Why did you come back, Ben?"

"Do you have to ask?"

"I want to hear you say it."

"What will saying anything achieve?"

"I want you to put it into words. I want ..." Painter shook his head. "I don't know, there's a finality about something once it's said. Tell me why this land has to be plunged into bloodshed and suffering. Tell me why the young men have to die. Tell me, I suppose, why I should be part of it."

"You don't have to be. You can go away tomorrow, right now if you wish. It's easy to forget."

"It's not my country," Painter said almost wistfully. "I'm a coward, I don't mind admitting it. I can't stand physical pain, or even discomfort. I was never one for causes or deep personal attachments. I've spent most of my life building up a professional cynicism against duty and remorse and even love."

Nzekwe shifted in his chair. He lifted two fingers at Painter, who grinned at him and said sheepishly, "It's as simple as that really, I suppose."

"Let me tell you something," Nzekwe said. "We got our independence too easily. There has to be bloodshed. The factors that have led to this are the old ones. It's as inexorable as time and the seasons. Only individual deaths will have any meaning, how you or I will die, that's all that matters."

"And how far and how deeply we allow ourselves to be pushed before we make a stand?"

"Perhaps. You must decide for yourself."

"And if a person puts himself in the position that he has to decide also for others?"

"Then he's either a fool or a madman."

23

"But you're advocating then that there should be no leaders. Are we all fit to know what's best for ourselves? In any crowd there is always someone who will get up and say, 'Look, here is the way. All you have to do is follow me.'"

"And why do they follow him?"

"Perhaps because he shouts the loudest. It often only takes a little confidence."

"The confident man is not always the wisest."

"Neither is he the one who must always be sneered at."

"I don't wish to deal in polemics tonight," Nzekwe said, suddenly angry and not bothering to hide it. "I want to get happily drunk. I want to forget."

"You told me yourself just a little while ago that it's easy to forget."

"And so it is. Only sometimes it needs a little help."

As if on cue, Nzendi suddenly came in with a bottle of beer under each arm. In his hands he carried a small radio from which a wheezy disembodied voice emanated, like someone crying for help from a long distance away. With an air of great importance he placed the radio on the table and then stood back and looked at them as if waiting for someone to pat him on the head. When neither Nzekwe nor Painter glanced at him he sat down on a chair a little way from then and folded his hands in his lap. He might have been a child waiting for his father to finish some meaningless conversation and to come and take him home.

The small scratchy voices on the radio rose and fell and sometimes a burst of music came through. Once, for almost a minute, there was a drum solo, like pebbles thrown against a window, and then the voices came back again, as tinny and indistinct as before. At a minute to twelve the voices ceased and there was a sound like someone breathing at the other end of a telephone. There was a hush in the room, and then the voice of Colonel Ojukwu came through, his heavy sad tones lending his words a solemn air, as he slowly and clearly pronounced the creation of Biafra:

"The territory and region known as, and called, Eastern Nigeria, together with her continental shelf, shall henceforth be an independent sovereign state of the name and title of the Republic of Biafra."

His voice faded away again, as if taken by the wind, and the sighing rustle of static returned. For some reason, Nzendi began to weep, the tears running through the powder of his face like snail track, and he got up and stood to attention. Painter opened his mouth as if he were about to speak, but suddenly Ojukwu's voice came back again, but fainter now. He was finishing the bulletin and his words whispered through the silence of the room:

"Long live the Republic of Biafra and may God protect all who live in her."

Suddenly Ben Nzekwe stood up. His head turned wildly from side to side as if he were looking for some way of escape, and a deep groan started deep inside him and then seemed to lodge somewhere in his throat. He picked up his half-empty bottle of beer and threw it at the wall, where it shattered against the portrait of the Queen, and then he ran from the room. Behind him, the radio began to play the new Biafran National Anthem.

3

The school at Ogundizzy covered the top and most of the sides of a small hill. The main school block, a two-storeyed white plaster rectangle, was the centrepiece, and the remainder of the buildings were thrown about haphazardly like the discarded toys of some careless giant. During the Wet Season erosion was always a problem, and blocks of cement steps had been built at various levels into the sides of the hill, but they in their turn were crumbling away like the hard laterite soil.

When Painter had first seen the hill, with its curious unfinished buildings, it reminded him of a hillside he had once seen in Athens; a hillside spotted with bare foundations, weed-choked altars, gap-toothed walls and huge monolithic blocks of stone; a hillside suspended in the timelessness of its historical actuality like smoke on a windless day. Ogundizzy Hill had no historical actuality, however, unless one counts the historical relevancy of the events of the day before yesterday.

Igor, the owner of the school and of most of Ogundizzy, believed that in order to get the ultimate out of his employees he should provide only the basic necessities of life, and these to him were four walls and a roof, a full belly once a day, and a woman once a week. He himself lived in the town, in a large sprawl of buildings which were in the same precarious state of disrepair as the houses of those who lived on the hill. Chief C.D.O. Igor, O.O.N., to give him his full title, was a very black blackman, with a face seamed

26

and fissured like the approach roads leading to his beloved hill. He was sixty-six years old, claimed to be fifty, and looked about forty. He had worked hard as a young man, as he never tired of telling anyone who cared to listen, and had never grown out of the habit. He looked upon himself more as a European than as an African – he was fond of declaring, "Those bloody blackmen, they don't know how to sweat" – for he admired the whiteman's capacity for work, and his organisational ability; and he viewed with scorn his fellow African's laziness and disinclination towards any form of ordered labour. Along with his elder brother, Stanislaus, whom he invariably referred to as "that fucking man", he ran his multifarious businesses in a welter of noise, confusion, and much impassioned shouting, always insisting that everything be written down, and sending memos couched in a high Victorian English to even the most illiterate of his employees.

He liked nothing better than an argument, slyly using any pretext for starting one, and then continuing on for hours in a loud harsh voice, often losing the thread of the discussion en route, and perhaps in the end finishing up by condemning what he had meant to praise. Most of these arguments took place in his airy sitting-room overlooking Ogundizzy Lake. In the evenings, at that time in the tropics when the sky becomes suffused by a soapy opalescence and, as a prelude to night, the air takes on a torpidity that is almost palpable, Igor would appear on the balcony of his house, slowly and solemnly, and would wave his arm like the conductor of an orchestra. Immediately the electric generator would start up, bringing to life the myriads of fairy lights that adorned the house. This sudden cascade of tiny twinkling lights never failed to please him, but if by chance the functionary who was in charge of this switching-on operation failed to come in on cue, as often happened, then Igor would be left on his balcony in lonely splendour, and with his kingdom drab and lightless about him. On such occasions he would go roaring off in search of his employee, but that unfortunate man had long since learned to absent himself as soon as he had pressed the switch.

After the ceremony of the lights, Igor would sit restlessly, awaiting his nightly parade of visitors. Some of them would come slinking in, bowing and scraping and unsure of their welcome; others, friends of his youth or business equals perhaps, would arrive boisterously, with much hand clasping and back slapping, but even they would thread warily until they were sure of Igor's mood. The kola nut would be broken and passed around, drink would flow freely, and Igor, always the centre of attention, would move about, sometimes ignoring his guests altogether in order to stride to the balcony and trade insults with whoever might be passing by below.

His wife would appear at some stage of the evening, a dignified, quiet woman of middle age, who knew very little English. Her appearance was perfunctory and she stayed only for a short time, smiling graciously and being greeted respectfully by all. She was Igor's show wife, the one who welcomed his guests and sat beside him in the first pew at Mass on Sundays. A number of her cousins also lived in the house, young nubile girls with pneumatic bodies who did no work and lazed about all day; they disappeared at various times, and if they returned, it was usually when Igor's wife had given birth to another of his innumerable children.

Igor professed to be a Catholic, and the man he most admired in Ogundizzy was Father Manton, who managed his school for him. And if the world had been searched over, a man better able to adapt himself to Igor's moods and fixations would not have been found, for Father Manton, being the antithesis of Igor, suited him like a glove. Igor would rant, Father Manton would smile and shake his head; and eventually Father Manton would do what Igor wished

28

or he would not, and whichever he did, it was usually what was needed in the first place.

The school was a good example of a co-operation between man and the angels: Igor made money out of it and the boys were given a type of education, while Father Manton saw to it that they observed the rites and ceremonies of the Catholic Church. On Saturday mornings Igor was permitted to use the student body as a free labour force, and the most common form of punishment given by the teachers was to send the erring student out to carry cement blocks.

There was no discrimination against any boy who wished to attend the school, providing that he had the money to pay the fees, was an Ibo and had a properly authenticated form to prove that he had been bapitised into the Catholic religion.

4

Painter wrote on the blackboard: "I am a simple man, a man with simple tastes. I have a small house in the bush, with a garden where I grow yam and kassava. One day a soldier came to my door and told me that I was wanted. I asked him what I was wanted for and he said that I was wanted to go and fight for my country ..."

He turned and looked at the rows of faces in front of him. This was Class One Alpha and it was their English period. He said, "Continue on where I have stopped and write a page on what you think should follow." He saw the puzzlement on their faces and he repeated what he had said, only more slowly and distinctly. It was always like this with the younger boys, it took them half the class before they could understand what he was saying, and each day he had to start all over again, repeating himself over and over, until he became frustrated and angry and could see the hurt and resentment in their puzzled brown eyes.

He walked about the room and watched them as they wrote, most of them forming the letters carefully and stopping often to think, for English was only their second language. They thought in Ibo and then had to translate their thoughts into English.

The room was a cubbyhole in the lower storey of the school building and two white-washed pillars formed barriers at each side of the room, so that small shaven heads were continually peering out at him whenever he spoke. Many of the desks were broken, and some of the boys had to share seats not spacious enough for one bottom, let alone two. One tiny boy in the front row had perfect European features and white skin, his father was French but he used his mother's name – Okatchu. He kept glancing about him, and whenever he caught Painter's eye, he smiled angelically, uniting the two of them in a conspiracy of uniqueness in the midst of so many black faces.

Painter sighed and sat down at his desk. He felt tired and he wished that the bell would ring. Dark clouds rested low upon the horizon, and overheard the sky had a colourless opacity like steam. The palm trees outside the window were tattered and lifeless, and breathing took a conscious effort. Another new building was being built at right angles to the one in which Painter had his class, and the men working on it were like slow motion figures labouring under water. Father Manton went by outside, a long stick-like figure in his white robes, and from somewhere overhead a voice cried out sharply as if its owner was in pain.

A sound in the class made Painter look up. Stephen Okatchu was standing up. "Yes?" Painter said.

"Have I permission to go outside to urinate?"

"No," Painter said automatically. He looked at his watch. "The bell will ring in another five minutes. You can wait until then."

The little boy sat down sullenly; Painter had let him down in front of the class. He had been trying for most of the year to establish a special relationship between himself and Painter, and each rebuff had only seemed to strengthen his resolve. He was one of the boys responsible for filling Painter's water tank, and he did twice as much as the others, carrying innumerable buckets of water on his head until it appeared that his small frame would buckle under the strain. He had made himself friendly with Jude, Painter's cook, and he hung about outside Jude's house in his leisure

31

time. When he returned from the Easter holidays, he brought a bottle of cheap Spanish brandy and presented it to Painter, together with two over-ripe mangoes. Painter had given the brandy to Jude and had thrown the fruit away.

The boys began to shuffle their feet, and Painter sent one of them around to collect the papers. Their starched white shirts and shorts, so clean and bright earlier in the day, were grubby and sweat-stained. The room smelled of chalk dust and perspiring bodies, and a seething line of soldier ants had appeared and was making its way busily across the floor in front of Painter's desk. Overhead a slow rumbling began, and when the bell rang stridently, Painter jumped as if he had not been expecting it.

The boys stood to attention for the usual prayer, but instead of crossing himself, Painter rubbed his face and said, "When you go outside, you are to line up just as you do for morning assembly. Father Manton has something to say to you." He paused and looked about him at the rows of serious young faces. He wanted to say something more, some word of farewell, but he had never been close enough to them in the past to presume now on their understanding. If he tried to speak to them to tell them how he felt, they would listen to him as they had always listened, with their heads and not with their hearts. He put out his hand and caught Stephen Okatchu by the shoulder, and he shook the boy gently as if trying to impress some point on him, but he had nothing to say. He waved them out and they went silently, two by two, their shaven heads bobbing against the bright reflected light, and behind them in the empty classroom Painter took the sheaf of uncompleted essays and, without glancing at them, threw them in the wastepaper basket.

Outside on the second-storey balcony the rest of the staff were standing and Painter went and joined them and leaned on the stone balustrade beside Kappel. Father Manton

32

stood below them, the boys forming up in front of him and watching his impassive face anxiously, wondering probably what they had done to make him look so stern.

"No one tells me anything," Kappel said. "I'm always the last to know what's happening." There was a tone of suppressed anger in his voice, and his face had a shiny bluish tinge, as if he had been drinking heavily the night before. Kappel was a large handsome Indian, and when he had first arrived in the school he had been a proud withdrawn figure, a Sikh in a white turban and with long greasy hair in a pigtail down his back. But one morning, about six months after his arrival, he had appeared minus his turban and with his hair dry and cut short, and he had called on Painter and greeted him as if he were meeting him for the first time. Kappel had a great pride in himself, and at first he had tried to impress Painter in various little ways; but Painter's silence had defeated him and he took to visiting him less and less. One night when he was drunk, he had come to Painter's window and had urinated in on him while he was asleep in bed. Painter had waited for three days and then had attacked him and opened a seven-inch wound in the back of his head with a hurley stick. They got along much better after that, for Kappel believed, in fact mistakenly, that Painter hated him, and that gave him a certain amount of satisfaction.

"They came last night," Painter said. "Two jeep loads of them. They are only the advance party, many of the students will enlist."

"How can they be so foolish?" Kappel said, leaning his elbows on the stone railing and watching Igor drive up to the front of the school in his battered red Volkswagen. "They will be submerged in a fortnight."

"They have a lot to fight for."

"What does it matter? What use is a land of dead heroes?"

Painter did not answer. He glanced about him at the

33

other teachers. The Africans were standing carefully, like soldiers at attention, and on their faces were the expressions of men who were afraid, but who were still determined to go on and do what they had to. They irritated Painter; they had no right to be so naive, while their world was preparing to collapse about them like a pack of cards. He looked down at Father Manton and wondered how he must be feeling. Twenty-five years of work and effort, sometimes misguided, but always well meant, he had spent his lonely years deep in the bush watching the seed he had planted flower, and in some cases grow strong. What use would their faith be to them now? Would it sustain them, make them die better?

The three soldiers came down the hill, walking smartly, their heads back, wide nostrils flared. But their shiny boots were mud-spattered, and the sunbursts on their shoulders looked dowdy in the grey light. Kappel laughed disparagingly, while the students shuffled their feet and Igor climbed out of his car. The scene was unreal to Painter, the silence too complete, the light too dull and diffused. He felt more of an outsider than usual. Kappel's anger gave him the right to be involved, but Painter felt nothing except a slight impatience. It was like a charade, an elaborate mime which, when it was over, would dissolve people in laughter, and both participants and onlookers would feel a great relief that it was in fact a game. Why is it that ridiculous events like the declaring of wars are always attended by such ceremonious solemnity? Painter wondered. Violent death is not a solemn occasion; it is horrible and grotesque, and ultimately meaningless to the person who has suffered it. How many people, Painter thought, have died cursing the person they have dived into a stormy sea, or walked across a minefield, to save?

One of the soldiers spoke first, a young man who was a past pupil of the school. He spoke unimpressively, talking of honour and glory and fighting for one's country, and fading away at the end into incoherence, as his emotions got the better of him. The school band played the Biafran National Anthem – "Land of the rising sun we love and cherish, Beloved home, land of proud heroes ..." – and Igor made a grudging speech, telling the students that they should enlist in the army and get the war over with as soon as possible.

When he finished, all eyes turned to Father Manton, as he stepped forward and cleared his throat. He was a tall, shy Irishman, from County Cork, and even after all his years in Nigeria he still retained the soft sibilants of his native accent. He was a bad speaker, his sermons in the town on Sundays being for the most part inaudible, and it was generally believed that his Ibo interpreter improvised as he went along. This morning his voice was lower than usual, and Painter missed the first few sentences. He seemed to be telling the boys to pack their possessions in time to leave the school on the following morning, as the whole compound was being taken over as a military camp.

His words came to Painter like words borne on and dying in a breeze, although there was no breeze. "Some of you will join the army, others of you will stay at home to take care of your families ... do not wish for you to go, nor did I wish for this war ... I know how terrible war can be, and I cannot, either in my own mind or to you, justify it ... perhaps such a thing as a just war, but so many individual acts of injustice occur because of man's inhumanity ... hate and bloodshed are nothing, even death is nothing, if your faith is strong enough ..." The words and phrases were old and stale, and frayed at the edges from too much repetition; they lacked conviction; they carried about them the echoes of too many despairs and futile aspirations. Painter remembered once, when he had asked Father Manton why he had become a priest, he had replied, "How do you answer a question like that? I was afraid, I suppose. I always carried

35

about with me a great fear of failing in my duty to God and to my fellow man, and I felt that becoming a priest might solve my problems," and when Painter had asked him if it had solved his problem, he had said, "Perhaps I made too big a gesture. Perhaps I gave too much all at one time. I sometimes feel that now I have nothing left to give."

Kappel broke in on Painter's thoughts – "He's giving them Christian ju-ju, now they'll rush at the enemy under the shield of heaven" – and Painter laughed, as if Kappel had indeed made a joke.

The boys began to fidget, and the orderly ranks of white-clad figures were no longer still, but merged and broke apart like the line of ants across Painter's classroom. Yet Father Manton's voice seemed to grow louder and more assertive, and his head was raised now, and he was gazing out over the lake as if he could see something that none of the rest of them could see. At first Painter did not understand, then he realised that the priest was quoting from St Paul – "What then shall we say to this? If God is for us, who is against us? Who shall separate us from the love of Christ? Shall tribulation, or distress, or persecution, or famine, or nakedness, or peril, or the sword? No, in all these things we are more then conquerors through Him who loves us. For I am sure that neither death, nor life, nor angels; nor things present, nor things to come; nor powers, nor height, nor depth, nor anything else in all creation, will be able to separate us from the love of God."

The students, hearing only the stirring words, gave a mighty cheer, and the young soldiers became so carried away that they hoisted the bewildered Father Manton onto their shoulders, and went jogging away across the compound, with his white-robed figure bobbing awkwardly up and down like a half-killed sack.

Kappel turned and laughed into Painter's face, but whatever he said was lost in the sudden roll of thunder which exploded like artillery fire in the sky overhead. The sound silenced the cheering crowd and, as the echoes died away, the boys were immobilised like figures in an old photograph, laughing faces, caught and held in their moment of hilarity like flies in amber. Only Father Manton moved, waving his arms about in the air as if he were imparting a blessing, and at the same time striving to keep his balance and prevent himself from falling from his ludicrous position on the shoulders of the soldiers.

Rain began to fall, grey rain from an angry sky.

5

It was dim in the hospital ward, glaucomatose electric light bulbs high up against the ceiling shedding a weak yellow lustre, yet the girl moved with a certain awkward grace between the children's beds. The starched nurse's uniform she was wearing gave her a flat-chested, boyish look, and the pale skin of her forehead had that achromatic, damp appearance which the tropics bestows on white complexions after only a short length of time. She hummed softly to herself as she walked.

All of the beds were occupied, some of them containing two children, one at either end. There was a continuous whimpering sound, which even the incessant clicking of the crickets in the darkness outside the open windows could not drown. The children, most of them the sons and daughters of refugees from distant parts of the region, were fretful. They were suffering from malnutrition and exhaustion, and some of them already exhibited the first signs of kwashiorkor. Some mothers lay on the floor beside their children's beds, and they too turned and muttered in their sleep, as if they suffered from bad dreams. There was little more they could do; they had already carried the children on their backs over miles of muddy road and flat, sodden bushland, only to see them now slowly die in the hard iron beds and among the antiseptic smells of Ogundizzy Hospital.

The girl stopped beside a cot which contained a brother and sister who had been brought in that afternoon. The children lay quietly, side by side; they were little more than large bony heads, with huge staring brown eyes. The girl laid her hand on the sheet and the spidery claw of the little girl closed about the index finger like the touch of a bird. If I could give them some of my life, the girl thought, it would only need a little, a tiny drop, to bring them back.

She disengaged her hand and went outside to where Painter was awaiting her. He was sitting on the raised stone verandah, his face in shadow, and a mosquito coil on either side of him spiralled thin ropes of smoke through the humid air. The girl sat down and Painter lit two cigarettes. He handed her one and she inhaled deeply on it, with an audible sigh.

"I've been thinking," Painter said. "We could drive over to Nwapa's. The road is clear again and it wouldn't take us more than half an hour to get there."

"I'm tired," the girl said. She passed her hand in front of her face as if she was brushing something away from her eyes.

"We could get drunk."

"We can do that here."

"Let's have a ball," Painter said, jumping up. He did a few slow turns in the gravel of the driveway, holding an imaginary partner in the circle of his arms. The girl laughed and joined him, and they whirled around and around, until they were both out of breath. Painter held on to her hand and pulled her round the corner of the building, where they were in darkness. He kissed her hard on the lips, and breathed into her mouth until she pulled away from him.

"Tonight, Anne?" he asked, putting his hands on her shoulders.

The girl stiffened, and even in the darkness he could sense the resistance that was in her. He tightened his hands on her shoulders into fists and leaned across her until his forehead was against the rough stone of the hospital wall. They stood like that until he broke away and walked back around the corner.

They sat and smoked in silence, an uncomfortable silence, a silence born of past misunderstandings and their mutual inability to break down inhibitions which of themselves had no real meaning. Painter was annoyed with the girl, yet he recognised in his annoyance how much he wanted her. If she would only fight him on his terms.

"Oh God," the girl said, "I hate this war."

Painter looked at her, but her face was in shadow, and all he could see was the glowing tip of her cigarette. "We all do," he said quietly.

"I hate it because it's breaking up a happy time. It's scattering people about like leaves in the wind. You'll have to go back home soon. Or I'll go."

"Then why shouldn't we be happy for a little time?"

"Could we?"

"Why not? All you have to do is to walk across the road with me; all you have to do is to say yes. It wouldn't take much effort."

"You don't want me enough."

"Want you enough! I want you more than anything else in this world. I dream about you, when I'm asleep and when I'm awake. I can't eat or read or even drink without thinking about you. Why do you think I stay up half the night waiting for you to be finished in this bloody hospital?"

"Perhaps you've nothing better to do."

Painter sighed. He said. "Anne, I've offered to marry you. What more do you want from me?"

"Yes, you've offered to marry me. Like a little boy saying to a little girl, 'I'll give you my catapult if you'll show me your knickers.' I'd probably have gone with you before now if you hadn't offered to marry me."

"But I love you."

"Do you? Do you really love me? You've told me enough times."

"What else can I do but tell you?"

40

"Force me? Knock me down and rape me if your desire is that big. You might even enjoy it."

"It's not just the physical side of it, Anne," Painter said. He sounded disapproving and the girl laughed, softly and mockingly.

"I feel like the well-defined centre of an imaginary circle," Painter went on. "You could provide something, a moment of fulfilment, something that I'd know is real. Otherwise I'm a non-man, or at least a dislocated one."

"Yet you love to talk about yourself."

"It's like picking at a sore."

"Strangely enough, some people enjoy doing that."

"Yes, as long as the sore is dried up and old and gives no more pain."

"That only happens when a wound is healed. And the presence of the sore predisposes the wound, and a wound is real."

"How do you know?"

"Because it bleeds, and because one feels pain. I treat wounds all day long, all kinds and shapes, big ones and small ones. I sew up limbs that look like the meat you see hanging on hooks in butchers' shops; I stuff back the prolapsed anus of a child who weighs no more than a feather and looks like a shrivelled monkey; and I have to watch that same child scream when I give him food, because it will be agony for him to pass it. As for shattered minds, I see them too and I can do nothing. These things are real, and so are the people. They don't have to go around sticking pins in themselves to know whether they are alive or not. If you want an excuse for your existence go out and find the war and die in it. It's an ideal opportunity."

Painter turned away from the girl and stood up. Over his shoulder he said, "I'd be afraid. It would have to come to me."

The girl also got to her feet. "I feel as if I'm living in a

41

thick cocoon of fetid cotton wool," she said. "The air, the atmosphere, the dreary people looking for sympathy and understanding. This should be a time of exhilaration. I wish the bombs would fall. Then we'd all be together, and the sense of danger might wipe away the indecision and the self-pity."

The lights in the ward behind them suddenly flickered and went out, but after a moment they came on again as the smaller generator, which was left on all night, was switched on. The girl put her hand on Painter's shoulder, but when he did not turn around, she walked down the steps and stood looking up at him. "I'm going to make some coffee," she said. "Why don't you walk me home?"

Painter stared down at her, then he stepped down into the gravel and took her hand. They moved out of the circle of light, and out past the white-washed walls of the convent. One of the Sisters was sitting on the verandah, and she murmured a soft goodnight like a benediction at them as they passed. Anne giggled and stepped into the circle of Painter's arm and put her head on his shoulder.

The nightwatch unlocked the door of the girl's house; he was an old man with large feet and a very bad skin disease, but in the darkness the livid patches on his face were hidden. He wore a rag, Arab fashion, about his head, and this disguised the fact that he had no ears. He was a Hausaman from the north of Nigeria, but he had lived so long among the Ibos that they had forgotten the fact.

While Anne made the coffee, Painter stood at the door and listened to the night sounds. There was no moon or stars, and the humidity in the air was heavy and palpable like the caress of a damp vapour. The wall under the outside light was crawling with insect life, and a sausage fly buzzed drunkenly about trying to immolate himself against the electric bulb.

The girl came in with the coffee and they switched on

42

the light while they were drinking it. A scatter of gecko lizards on the wall froze in the sudden brilliance, and Painter grimaced as the scalding coffee burned his tongue.

"They become so afraid that their hearts burst," Anne said.

"What?"

"The lizards. If you frighten them, they die of a heart attack. And if you try to catch them by the tail, the tail comes away in your hand."

"They're very beautiful, like windflowers."

"I hate them." The girl hunched down in her chair. She looked exhausted, her hair lay damply against her forehead and her hand shook as she lifted the cup to her lips.

"You're working too hard," Painter said. "You should take siesta, or at least get to bed earlier at night."

"Do you remember the last time we went to Port Harcourt? How we bought doughnuts in Kingsways, and afterwards we drank too much and you got sick in the swimming pool at the European Club?"

"You got so angry when they asked us to leave. You almost killed the secretary with the carved head you had bought in the market."

"He was a very rude man."

Painter got up and switched off the ceiling light. He pulled his cane chair over to where the girl was sitting and sat down beside her; but from somewhere in the hospital there came the wild ululation of keening women, and as suddenly as a shower of tropical rain, it dispelled the mood that had grown up between them.

"Another child is dead," Anne said. She put her cup carefully on the floor. "It's such a waste," she went on angrily, "and there are so many dying. Only a fraction of them are brought in, the bush swallows up the rest. There's nothing to signify their passing, not even sorrow."

"Death in great numbers never has any meaning. When

43

someone that one knows dies there is sorrow, or rage, or perhaps even fear. When many people die, it should only be read about in the newspaper, or heard over the radio. It's a statistic to be recorded and filed away somewhere in a dusty room."

"All this talk about death ..."

"I think that everyone is allotted a certain store of words and actions, and they must be rationed carefully so that they will last a lifetime."

"And if death comes too soon?"

"Then someone else will say and do the things for you. There is always continuity."

"You speak as if people came off a conveyor belt, as if their thoughts and feelings were routine and all alike."

"Yes, like a record going round and round. When the needle slides off the playing surface, there is silence; and when the arm is put back to the beginning, the same things will merely be said again and again."

The girl turned her head and peered at Painter. "What are we talking about?" she said in a tone of suppressed anger. "We're not dead. We can still hurt one another. We can talk, or sing, or dance; we could tell one another jokes, and we could say things that we really mean ..."

"Even if they weren't true?"

"Yes, why not? How are we to be sure unless we try? You could continue telling me you loved me, and out of all the times, there might be once when I'd believe you."

"I love you, I love you, I love you ..." Painter spoke as if he had been given some order relating to his duty as a lover.

"Why did you stop?"

"You're asking too much of me. I might as well say that I don't love you. If you could be satisfied with what I'm willing to give ..."

"But you've given me nothing."

44

"Christ Almighty, what do you want? Do you want to flay me? Do you want my skin as a trophy?"

"I want you to tell me once, and mean it, that you love me."

"I can't, I haven't got that kind of courage. And yet it's there, if I could only reach it."

"Like a retreating waving hand?"

"Now you're laughing at me."

"If so, it's dark laughter. At the very first operation I attended I laughed too. But afterwards I cried all night."

Painter went over to the door and put his face against the coolness of the glass. The nightwatch appeared at the other side and looked in at him. The old man's face was pitted and scarred like the side of a hill, and Painter half expected to see ants crawling in and out of the cavities. When he raised his hand, Painter started back from the anticipated greeting, but the old man had not seen him, and was merely reaching up to pick some insects off the wall outside. He put them in his mouth and chewed them as if they were a rare delicacy.

"Will I see you tomorrow night?" Anne said.

"Why not." Painter opened the door, and then he paused and looked back at the girl, but he could barely see her in the dimness. "Goodnight," he said, but there was no answer, and he slowly closed the door behind him and walked back up the gravel path towards the hospital.

6

Painter dreamed of snow-capped mountains and thin cold air whining in his lungs like wine. It was a dream that had haunted him since he had come to Nigeria. Sometimes the mountains were in the far distance, mistily there on the horizon, while a heavy sea surged and heaved like a plain of grey wrinkled lava. Seals broke the surface of the sea, sleek and glistening, and there was a turgid roll and swell as if the whole world was wallowing on its axis.

It was usually during siesta that Painter dreamed. He slept fitfully, in a welter of sweat, and he often grew confused, so that he did not know if he was asleep or awake. He was afraid to sleep too long in the afternoons, for then he would lie awake at night, alone in the darkness, listening to the sounds outside his window and, if the moon was out, watching the shifting patterns of shadow as they moved across the ceiling. Now in the Wet Season it was better, for the rain obliterated all the night sounds, and it was often quite cool, with sometimes a wind blowing through the open windows. He could have stopped taking siesta, but there was nothing else to do. Reading was a habit he had grown out of and no one moved about the compound at that hour. During the Dry Season he had tried going down to the lake. He sat in the front of a canoe, while the old woman who had it for hire paddled slowly and laboriously, and the unwieldy bulk moved across the shimmering brilliance. The world then shrank to a microcosm, a frightening claustrophobia of self, where thoughts and images became fragmented, became spots of iridescence in his mind like the sun breaking on the ripples of water. Painter had allowed his mind to become disused, the slow cycle of life in Africa suited him, but out on the lake in the stark afternoon sun he became frightened, for there he had no place to hide, there he had to think of time wasted, of trivialities dressed up and disguised as events of importance. There had been so many things to be done and so many opportunities for words to be said, and yet he had said and done nothing, and the chances had been lost. It was so difficult in the artificial atmosphere, in the closed intense society in which he moved, to know what was indeed truly felt, and what was merely the product of the time and the place. It was similar to his moments of waking and sleeping: he could not be sure, and so he did not want to be sure. So he had stopped going out on the lake, and instead he spread a towel under his head and lay on his bed and dreamed.

He turned onto his side and picked up his watch from the chair beside the bed. It was only three o'clock, and today even the sounds of the boys moving down to the river for their afternoon swim were missing. He lay back, little pools of sweat gathering immediately in the hollows of his neck, and the mattress, still in its cellophane covering, squeaked as he moved.

It was a week now since the soldiers had entered the compound. They had been most apologetic about disturbing him. A young handsome Ibo officer had come to his door at six in the morning and Painter had talked to him through the open louvres of his bedroom window. All the time they had talked, the young man had smoothed what was probably a new growth on his upper lip. He told Painter that his commanding officer, a Colonel Ozartu, had sent his greetings, and would Painter come and see him as soon as he had the time.

"You don't remember me?" the officer had asked Painter.

47

"You look familiar, perhaps I taught you ... ?

"I did a teacher training course here last year. You remember the night your friend stole your car?"

Painter remembered him then, a quiet serious young man who wanted to get on but was prepared to remain a teacher. Many of the others had used teaching as a stepping stone to other, more lucrative posts.

"I'm afraid we were rather drunk that night," Painter said. "I don't believe I ever really apologised to you ..."

"There was no need, it was of no consequence. I was glad that your friend did not injure himself or your car."

"He acted foolishly. He often did things like that when he was drunk." Painter himself had felt foolish remembering O'Rourke, but at the time it had seemed a wild and dangerous night.

Later that morning Painter had walked about the compound and watched how self-consciously the newly constituted soldiers performed their various tasks. Many of them were boys who had been his students a short while before. They smiled uncertainly at him and smoothed their starched fatigues, but they were doing the same old things, carrying blocks, transporting buckets of water on their heads, and it was almost as if nothing had changed. Was the art of soldiering and of preparing for war so mundane? Painter wondered. Did a soldier eat and drink and defecate, did he make love, and was the actual killing the climax in his life, the moment comparable to the time when the businessman clinched the biggest deal, or the gambler brought off the greatest coup, or the priest held the host in his hands for the first time? Did killing become easy after a time, just like everything else?

He had sat on the school steps and looked down on the lake, where the fishermen sat patiently astride their reflections. The war was approaching over the tops of those distant hills, but it was still inaudible and unseen. Only the increasing stream of emaciated refugees from the West and the Mid-West bore testimony to the tragedy that was being played out along the Niger and in the scrubland around Ogoja. The radio broadcast nothing but martial music and a stream of propaganda of World War Two vintage, using phrases like "bore strategic losses", "organised withdrawal", or "the enemy is being routed on all sides", and the peculiar African inflection invested the words with the inhuman tones of a science fiction serial.

When the Colonel in charge had sent for him a second time, Painter had gone to see him. He sat in what had been Father Manton's office, a bare room containing a badly made desk and some straight chairs. There were pictures around the walls, group photographs of students and football teams, many of them faded and brown like old daguerreotypes from the distant past. The office, despite its austerities, had always been a place to relax in, for Father Manton had the gift, peculiar to many quiet people, of being able to disseminate goodwill without having to work too hard at it.

Colonel Ozartu had made very few changes, the desk was a little neater, Father Manton's solar topee, his "relic of old decency" as he called it, no longer hung on the wall, but the picture of the Pope remained, and he had been joined by the brooding visage of Colonel Ojukwu, the heavy face, so vulnerable to caricature, already expressing a deep sadness.

"Thank you for coming, Mr Painter," Colonel Ozartu had said. "Perhaps you would like some beer?"

Painter shook his head, sitting there in that office with a glass in his hand would bring back too many memories. He felt that the Colonel was waiting for him to speak, so he said, "I find that when I drink beer early in the day it makes me drowsy. Or it makes me depressed."

"You must find it difficult now to occupy your time."

Painter was not sure if the Colonel's remark was a statement or a question. He said, "The time passes, I'm good at doing nothing."

The Colonel smiled. He was a heavy man, who filled his freshly-pressed uniform well. The collar of his shirt was open and the skin of his neck and jaws was rough-noduled and shiny. He must have found shaving painful, perhaps he would soon grow a beard like his leader. "Would you like me to find something for you to do?" he asked. "Many of my troops cannot even write their own names."

"Is that so necessary? It might only confuse them."

"The majority of them are farmers, or boys from the towns who had no work anyway. War gives employment to all."

"It must be hard to know what to pay people to die for you."

"Some will die, but even the Church recognises the need for sacrifice."

"They are simple men, why complicate their lives? If I taught them to write then they would want to read; then perhaps they would begin to think."

"You believe that there is no place in an army for the thinking man?"

Painter sighed. He said, "It's too early in the morning for questions like that. And besides, what answer can I give you that would satisfy you? Would you like me to say that war, and the waging of it, can be an intellectual exercise, that like the Japanese Samurai a soldier can make a religion out of his profession? But you are a professional soldier, you don't need justification, or equivocation for that matter, about something which is so everyday to you."

"Simple men," Colonel Ozartu said musingly. "It's easy to inspire them now. Later it will not be so easy."

"You have no chance of winning, you know. It's a futile gesture."

"A gesture." Colonel Ozartu stood up and walked to the

50

window. "You regard it as a gesture," he said over his shoulder. "Eight million people may die, may be completely wiped off the face of the earth, and you regard it as a gesture." He turned and faced Painter, but he did not appear to be angry.

"I didn't mean it like that. The implications are terrible, the actuality is unspeakable, but is it necessary? Gowan is a reasonable man, he would have compromised." Painter was thinking aloud, rather than conducting a dialogue with the Colonel. He remembered how Ben Nzekwe had said almost the same words, and at the time he had disagreed with him. What had happened to make him change his mind? Was it the sight of his former pupils so innocently shedding their youth? Or was it nostalgia for the places and things and way of life he had known now for over four years?

"Mr Painter," Colonel Ozartu said, "you sound bitter. Why do you stay? All the others, except doctors, nurses and Fathers, have gone. You must be almost the last teacher left."

Painter was to be asked that same question many times. It was the right question, but he had no answer for it. To Colonel Ozartu he said, "Perhaps that is my reason, I want to be the last. It's like the captain being the only one left on a sinking ship, or the pilot down with his plane, it has a certain element of the heroic."

But Painter knew that the captain and the pilot had a duty, a tradition, above all, a reason, for doing what they did. He had none, not even a great love of the people or the land. He had liked the people, but that was not love, and the land had always been an infinite source of small discomforts and irritations. Most of the expatriates, even the Fathers, referred to some other place as home. West Africa offered no fertile soil to the seeds of need and belonging which foreigners tried to sow.

Painter had left the office when the silences had grown embarrassing. He liked the Colonel, and in a normal time

51

they would have found plenty to talk about. They understood each other to a certain extent, but only on a superficial level, like men who worked together but at night went home to opposite ends of a city.

7

In late June, Painter and Father Manton travelled into Na'wadi to see the Bishop. The bush road was choked with people even though it was not yet first light. It was too dangerous to travel by daylight, the planes had already begun their erratic raids, dropping their bombs as if in a hurry to be rid of them, and then staggering away drunkenly over the tops of the palm trees. The pilots usually chose to drop their lethal cargoes on market places; bombs were very expensive and they had to be as effective as possible. The first time Ogundizzy market had been bombed Painter had gone down with his boy Jude to view the scene. The plane had dropped three bombs in a diagonal line across the market. Two of them had exploded, but in the already tilted leanings and general carelessness of the bambam shelters, little damage seemed to have been done. People drifted about, or stood alone with bemused expressions on their faces, and even the chattering of the weaverbirds had become stilled. Fragmented scenes remained in Painter's mind: a pregnant woman sliced open by a piece of shrapnel lying on a cord mat, the foetus visible and coiled like a question mark in the bloody ruin of her shattered belly; a young boy, whose arm had been blown off, sitting on a stool among his relatives and holding the bloody stump away from him as if he was afraid that the blood might stain his white shots; Father Manton looking like a butcher while administering the last rites to a jumbled pile of limbless torsos. Painter felt completely and utterly useless; the people seemed glad that he was there, they came up to him and touched him, but he only wanted to be somewhere else, not just away from the sight and smell of death but out of the country altogether. He had no words of consolation to offer to the old men who gazed hopefully at him from under the brims of their hats, he had no love to extend to the sorrowing women and he had no anger to share with the young people. Like love, grief also demanded involvement, and responsibility, and above all, a sense of belonging. Painter felt nothing.

Now as the car bumped along the dirt road he shifted in his seat, and his shirt came away stickily from the upholstery of the car. The light from the headlamps was diffused by the early morning greyness and the people at the sides of the road loomed up indistinctly like badly-sketched charcoal drawings. When the sun came up the roads would be deserted, the people cowering in their houses with nothing to do, farmers staring out at their unplanted patches of land and the children playing at being soldiers. It was so changed from what it used to be, when a journey by car along a bush road was like a minor triumphal procession, with little naked boys and girls waving and crying, "Fada," or "Beke," and the women carrying immense loads on their heads like outrageous hats. The whitemen were kings of the land, bringing prosperity and education, it was a status symbol to know them. The Fathers held a special position, the people did not understand them – they seemed to be willing to give without taking anything in return, but Painter and O'Rourke, the only two white teachers in Ogundizzy, were different. They drank and fornicated and in the extroversion of their Irishness resembled to a great extent the Ibos themselves. Not that Painter had ever been accepted, he had always lacked confidence in the making and breaking of friendships and at first he had been accused of being proud. To deny this he had started going to the native hotels and buying drinks for everyone, until finally the demands made on him were so great that one night he had become monumentally drunk and had smashed a bottle of Kai-kai on the cement floor of the Welfare Hotel. Setting light to it with a flourish, he had kept everyone out and watched one of the proprietor's shoes being consumed in the sea of blue-white flames. He had threatened to take a sample of the alcohol to Enugu to have it analysed and the sincerity of his anger had swept away most of the contempt which the villagers had for him so that when he again appeared among them he had won a grudging toleration.

But it did not really matter, for the main part of Painter's time and socialising was spent in the company of other Europeans. They were small in number but still they were clearly broken up into distinct groups. The Irish, both lay and clerical, spent their time in the bush, but it was genteel bush, not the isolation and Rivers country of the oilmen and the big construction company workers. By the time that Painter had arrived in Nigeria in the early sixties most schools and missions had their own generators, kerosene powered fridges, running water, film projectors; many of the roads were tarred, and even the smaller towns had coldstores and cinemas. Painter had come four thousand miles in search of a new lifestyle, in search of something strange and unfamiliar, and he had settled into a society no different from the one he had left. He took tea in the morning and at six in the evening, he employed a cook who had been trained by the nuns to serve bacon and cabbage and stodgy apple dumplings in the heat of a tropical noon, he entertained his Irish friends and read month-old Irish newspapers, and he went to Mass most mornings for, although he was not particularly pious, breaking the habit would require explanations and withdrawal. He tried to be a good teacher but the boys he taught posed no problems, they asked no questions. They were the lucky ones, and they accepted his teaching, not because it broadened their minds and stirred their aspiring hearts, but because it was a valuable commodity, because it could be used to gain position and material things and ultimately, perhaps, power. He never talked to them because, once his words transcended the pragmatism of the school course, a hiatus developed that was filled only with silence and meaningless smiles. He had tried to talk about this with O'Rourke, for they had come out together and had been friends for a long time, but he had the same difficulty and could find no solution either.

The bush road ended and the car bumped out onto the strip of wet tar. Painter shook himself free of his thoughts like a dog shivering off water and said, "I find it difficult to sleep lately. I doze a lot." It sounded like an excuse for his long silence.

"No one sleeps well anymore," Father Manton said. He shifted gear noisily. He had never learned how to drive properly, it was not indispensable to the business of saving souls.

"Do you remember when we drove down to Uzuable to find Omeke?" Painter said. "It was at this time in the morning, it was a Saturday, I think. Everyone thought we were mad."

Father Manton chuckled. "We proved them wrong," he said. "He won the match for us."

"I wonder were we wrong? Giving him a football scholarship, I mean. I never saw him again after we had won the cup."

Painter looked out of the window of the car. It was full light now but the clouds were low in the sky and the chill of dawn was still in the air. Soon the Wet Season would be over and the roads would dry up, and a curtain of red dust would drift in the air like smoke. The road was only tarred in the centre and the laterite at the edges was either a morass of mud or a stretch of rutted concrete, depending on the season. An army jeep approached them and passed in a slash of muddy water, and then the road was clear and deserted in front of them again.

"I met him last week," Father Manton said.

Painter was startled, he had lost the thread of their conversation. "Who?" he asked.

"Omeke. He was putting down stakes in the square at Na'wadi. He asked after you."

"It seems so long ago ..."

"It's only two years, that's not so long."

"Perhaps."

They slowed down for the dangerous curve at Osuiji. It was here, many years before, that the villagers had taken the taxi driver from the sanctuary of the priest's house and stoned him to death for knocking down a child. When they found that the child was only slightly injured, the people had become afraid and had killed him also.

Further along the road a man sitting in a towcart in front of a Ju-ju shrine waved at them as they went past. He was the guardian of the shrine, an outcast, a sacrifice to the god of that particular place. At his birth his legs had been smashed to prevent him from running away and now he sat and watched the cars and the people go by, and waited for death to come and take him away.

Painter glanced at Father Manton. He took a breath and said, "I suppose the Bishop wants me to leave." They had avoided the subject up to then.

Father Manton looked embarrassed. "Perhaps it would be for the best," he said.

"Did you ask him to talk to me? I won't go unless you actually order me."

"Neither he nor I can order you to go, we can only advise you. You were employed by the government. You still are, I suppose."

"I came out through the Mission ..."

"Are you claiming our protection? We can only give you spiritual aid."

"A kind of third party policy?" Painter said. He laughed and lit two cigarettes. He handed one to Father Manton.

"Something like that. But the air strikes are getting worse and they cannot withstand many more attacks on Onitsha."

"Do you know why I want to stay? You've never asked me."

"I suppose it's because of Anne ..."

"Not entirely. Tell me, why do you stay?"

"That's different, we have rules of obedience." Father Manton flicked ash out the open window, but it whipped back in and settled in a grey cloud on his white soutane.

"That's no answer, you could go if you wanted to."

"We have work to do here."

"That's to say that I have none. Is my work in the hospital not useful? Do you not need me for the Bridge school?

Father Manton did not smile. He said, "Those are unimportant things to risk losing your life for."

"I'm not brave, Father," Painter said, "and I don't want to die. I'm curious. I don't want to leave something which may never happen to me again."

"There will always be wars."

"Yes, but not on one's very doorstep. If I leave now, I may in the future have to search for another. And that might be too much of an effort."

"I don't understand you," Father Manton said querulously. "I've known you now for four years, yet you've never told me anything about yourself. O'Rourke always brought me his problems, but you ..."

"That's one of the drawbacks of being a priest, Father, you become after a time a professional confessor."

"You mean we lose the human touch?"

"You begin to put people into compartments. You hear so many troubles that their solutions become too obvious to you. I think you forget that each worry is individually his to each person. There is no easy solution, ever. I don't even know what my problem is, so how can I present it to you to be solved?"

"Perhaps you haven't got any problems. Perhaps that is your problem, the lack of one."

Painter gestured aimlessly in the air with his right hand. He said, "I suppose it's part of man's sin, the need to worry. But I'm worse than most, I can fool myself too easily; and that can leave an emptiness that can become impossible to fill. I think everyone comes up against one big test in life. The difficulty is in recognising it and not letting it slip past unnoticed."

"If that is what you believe then your life must be filled with terror."

"Not terror, Father. Disappointment."

Painter stared straight ahead of him through the windscreen of the car and soon the framework of the cathedral at Na'wadi loomed up in the distance. "It's strange," he said musingly, "how a Church which is based on the idea of God's spiritual kingdom keeps raising so many monumental roof-trees in order to impress its members. Is it a sop to people's need for security ... that God too should have a fine house?"

Father Manton shrugged his shoulders. "People must be impressed," he said vaguely.

The car came to the outskirts of Na'wadi and went across the bridge and past the Rest House, where the two old watchnights were already in position, two ancient men as faded and useless as Christ's sleepy disciples. Down the hill and right at the roundabout and the Bishop's house was in front of them, nestling in the shadow of the cathedral like a chicken under the wing of a hen. They drove in along the gravel driveway and drew up in front of the house where the Bishop was standing surveying his roses. He was a large man, much too heavy and fat for the climate, who usually smelled of stale sweat and tobacco smoke. Painter always thought that he would have looked more at home in a farmyard, wearing Wellington boots and swearing perhaps at a recalcitrant tractor.

"I've been in this country for sixteen years," he said as they got out of the car, "and I've never succeeded in growing a proper rose. I've spent a fortune on them and look what I'm left with." He pointed his finger and they stood and gazed at the etiolated flowers drooping wearily from olive-green stems. "They haven't even the energy to grow thorns," the Bishop said. "They disgust me."

"Why don't you grow something else?" Painter asked him. "The African flowers can be beautiful."

"It's the challenge, I suppose. Someone told me once that it's impossible to grow roses in this climate. I've been trying to prove him wrong ever since."

They walked up and down in the meagre garden. Two black Brothers came out of the building which had once housed the printing press, and when they saw the Bishop they stopped talking and smiled at him like guilty children. Father Manton excused himself and wandered self-consciously away, and the Bishop said, "I miss the people calling. There was a time when I hid from them. They came in droves. You would not believe the things they wanted, most of them full of indignation, and endlessly talking. Once an old man insisted on seeing me, and when the holy nuns finally allowed him in he became so frightened that he urinated on my best carpet."

"What did he want?"

"I never did find out."

They continued walking. The Bishop walked heavily, a

fat man's walk, his feet turned out and his shoulders and arms moving, in, out, in, as if they were dragging him along. His soutane was muddy about the bottom and two of the top buttons were undone, revealing the collarless neck of a grey shirt. Painter had always been uneasy in the man's presence; it was not the man himself but what he stood for, the ceremony of kissing the ring, of referring to him as "My Lord", it made Painter angry that he could still be influenced by the awe and the reverence.

"You wanted to see me?" Painter said, and the abruptness of his question plainly dismayed the Bishop.

"Yes, I sent for you," he said. "I want you to help me." He spoke jovially, yet there was something evasive about him, a certain set rigidity of the jaw muscles, as if he had to clamp his teeth together to prevent himself from saying the wrong thing.

"How?"

"I want you to go to Ireland and help us from that end. Speak to the people. Tell them how it is out here."

"How it is ..."

"Yes, the Irish love missionaries. I remember when I was a little boy there used to be a collection box in the local hardware store. It was for the Black Babies. It had a figure fixed to it which nodded its head every time a coin was dropped in. I often put buttons in to see the head nod."

"Why is everyone so concerned about me?" Painter suddenly said, a note of petulance in his voice. "I don't present any danger to you. I'll sign a paper if you like to say that if anything happens to me it is my own fault. I'm looking for something and I'll go when I find it."

"From what little I've seen of you I would have thought that you were a cynical man. Only an idealist would expect to find what he is looking for."

"You misunderstand me. What I'm looking for is not a beginning or an end. I'm seeking something small, a valid

61

gesture, a trivial act, an experience ..." Painter stopped in the middle of the garden as if he had forgotten where he was going. "As long as it's real," he said.

"Real!" For the first time the Bishop sounded irritable. "Is the reality of what is happening here not real enough for you?"

"It doesn't touch me. I only hear, I cannot see or feel. It's as if someone had come from a long way and told me stories of what was happening in a distant land." Painter paused and then, almost in a pleading voice, he said, "I'm thirty-two years old and I don't ever remember having been young. Look at my hands, they're the hands of an old man. But there must have been a time ... The years slip by and you don't notice them, and you wonder how you have so many aches and pains. I never did anything with my youth. I ran no races, scaled no mountains. The girls I knew, my school-friends, they left no impression. There should be one or two memories, something that I alone know about, something that could bring me back and make me see myself as I was then." He stopped and looked at the Bishop, but he did not see him. "And yet I suppose I had a happy childhood," he went on. "There was no pain, no loss, no one in my family ever seemed to die. There was a certain amount of fear, but it was fear of small things, of being alone in the dark, fear of sights and sounds and people ..."

Painter's voice trailed away and he looked up when the Bishop put out his hand as if to stop him from going any further, but there was no place further for them to walk, for the garden ended just then. The Bishop said, "It's not easy, but I still don't think there's anything for you here. What can you do?"

Painter looked at the wilderness of bush in front of him. He said, "You try to grow roses because someone told you it's impossible. One keeps on trying, it's not easy to give in."

"It's not a question of giving in, it's a question of coming to terms with oneself. I once imagined myself as the St Patrick of Africa. Now I'll be glad to die at home in Ireland."

They walked back to the front of the house, to where Father Manton was standing reading his Office. As Painter got into the car the Bishop said to him, "Come and see me again. Come and see me when you realise that compromise is not necessarily bad or weak, but is merely part of the human condition. And who knows, perhaps my roses will be in bloom when you come."

8

The days went by, and weeks, and the Wet Season wore itself out in a last flourish of dazzling storms. General Gowan appointed twelve civilians as members of a Federal Executive Council to administer the states into which he had divided Nigeria. The identity of the twelfth man, who was to represent the East Central State, was kept secret.

At first the war went well for the Biafrans; they even managed to break out of their own territory and invade the Mid-West. Benin was taken and the road to Lagos was open, but due to a combination of conspiracy and lack of proper communications the invasion faded out. Ojukwu had to execute a number of his officers, and one of the best of his field commanders, a young man like himself who had been one of the main instigators of the original coup, was shot by his own men while out on night patrol. Federal forces began to attack by sea, and Bonny and Opobo, the old slave trading towns on the Bight of Biafra, were under siege. In October Enugu fell.

Refugees began to pour into the interior of the new republic. The population of the main towns of Aba, Owerri and Umuahia were swelled to bursting point; the seasonal harvest was not sufficient to feed the increased number of people; and a flourishing black market shot up the price of food. People stalked the ubiquitous flying ants; lizards were caught in all kinds of ingenious ways, rats were butchered and sold as delicacies, and the last few remaining snakes, even the sacred Eke, were killed and eaten.

In Ogundizzy Father Manton started a co-operative to grow rice at the edge of the lake, and as the first Christmas of the war approached the morale of the people was still high. Only Igor complained, he looked upon the war as a personal insult to himself: it prevented him from getting on with his various businesses, it left his lorries and his workers idle, and it gathered into Ogundizzy hordes of his relatives from all parts of the region. They swarmed in, surrounding his house with their rickety bambam shelters, slaughtering his few carefully nourished cattle, and packing themselves so tightly into his sitting-room that one evening his outside balcony collapsed under the weight of half a dozen of them and dropped them screaming into the street below.

Igor's brother, Stanislaus, was one of the first casualties of the war. He was returning one afternoon from Aba with three thousand pounds in a black satchel tied to his wrist, when a crowd of renegade soldiers stopped the car and demanded the money. When Stanislaus refused to give them the key of the lock they shot him in the foot, cut his hand off at the wrist and disappeared into the bush with the satchel and the hand. The driver of the car went with them. When Igor heard of what had happened he went to the hospital carrying a machete and tried to force his way in, in order to "cut that fucking man's other hand off".

But for Painter nothing changed. He continued to see Anne Siena, they drank coffee and talked, and they slowly grew further and further away from each other. During the day he did odd jobs about the hospital, and taught listless groups of soldiers how to read and write. He read innumerable books, often having to stop in the middle of a chapter and turn back to the beginning because he had lost the thread of the story. As the Dry Season became hotter he found it more and more difficult to concentrate. He took to visiting the Welfare Hotel in the afternoons, where he drank Kai-kai with the owner, Adolphus, and the serving boys, Martine and Joseph.

In Christmas week Painter drove into Owerri, but the town was closed tight like a clenched fist. The people were grim and shabby, the bars and the hotels sold only watered Golden Guinea beer and the clock at the roundabout had stopped at a quarter to three. The Rest House had been taken over by army officers, and when Painter tried to drive in he found that the carpark was studded with bamboo stakes set solidly in the ground about a foot apart, and looking for all the world like accusing fingers pointing at the sky. One of the old nightwatches who remembered him from other times told him that the Federals were going to come out of the skies and take the town while the people slept.

Painter went to see Ben Nzekwe who lived in a house near the open air cinema. He shared it with four other families, and a small army of naked children clamoured at Painter's heels as he approached the door. Nzekwe had one small windowless room, which was redolent with a heavy odour of urine and stale sweat. The room contained two hard wooden chairs, a spirit stove and a fire-blackened mattress; a table leaned precariously against one wall, and in a corner stood a garishly painted portrait of John F. Kennedy. Nzekwe was sitting on one of the chairs drinking cheap wine straight from a bottle. He grinned at Painter when he came in and gestured at a row of full bottles standing on the table. Painter raised his hand in acknowledgement, took one of the bottles and sat down on the other chair.

They drank for a time in silence, and then Nzekwe began to pace up and down, chain smoking and waving his hands about as if he had to clear a path for himself through the fetid air. He talked about the latest news from the warfront – "They say there were over a hundred trucks. When the first one went it started a chain reaction which blew up the remainder. Like a string of firecrackers ... The soldiers are keeping it like a shrine, it's a holy place to send pilgrims to" – and all the time that he talked, a child in some other part of the house cried in a thin plaintive whine.

Painter shifted creakingly in his chair. The room was stifling and he was covered in sweat as if he had just taken a shower. Outside, the voices of the children were shrill, and a car door banged making Painter wonder if it was his own.

"It's almost Christmas," Nzekwe said. "Last year it snowed in London. The lake near where I lived was frozen over. I walked out on it and the ice groaned under my weight. Someone shouted at me that it was dangerous, but I stayed out there for a long time. It was very cold ... later that day I picked up a girl but she was as thin and cold as the ice."

"What are you doing now, Ben?" Painter asked. His voice sounded strange to him, as if he were talking in an echo chamber.

"I'm writing propaganda for the government. Would you like to hear a sample?"

"Why not."

Nzekwe took up a fresh bottle and drank from it and then handed it to Painter. The wine was dry and resinated and it burned the throat like vinegar. Painter gagged on it, but he forced it down as it was beginning to make him drunk. "What about this deathless prose of yours?" he said.

Nzekwe picked up a sheet of paper from the table and began to read: "On the evening of the fourteenth of December last a patrol of the First Division of the Biafran Army, led by Lieutenant Pius Osu, infiltrated the enemy lines at Kerdem. They were on a search and destroy mission." Nzekwe paused and looked at Painter. "I got that last sentence from *Time* magazine," he said slyly.

"You're a simple man, Ben," Painter said. He smiled at Nzekwe, a vacant drunken smile.

"Lieutenant Osu is a typical soldier of the glorious Biafran Army," Nzekwe went on, "a short lean young man with an open boyish face and shrewd eyes. Before the war started he was attending his Higher School course at Nwarbu Secondary School, where he was studying Mathematics and Physics. When the war broke out he did not hesitate, but immediately joined the army, and after a six weeks training session he was made a second lieutenant and was sent to fight at Nsukka. Up to the evening of the fourteenth of December he had distinguished himself in action on no fewer than five occasions, once single-handedly taking on a full patrol of Federal troops and wiping them out completely. His men adored him and would have followed him without question into any situation, no matter how suicidal."

"The fourteenth of December was a brilliant day, a bottomless pale blue sky giving an impression of depth and distance to the flat countryside around Kerdem, and when evening came, it seeped in almost imperceptibly like a soft thickening of shadow. The soldiers of the First Division who were defending the old town welcomed the approaching darkness, for it would afford them a respite in the almost continuous fighting. They were tired and sore as they moved through the clouds of red dust, which they had deliberately stirred up to hide them from the enemy. The Federals would not attack again until dawn.

"Lieutenant Osu was as tired as the rest, but he had been given his orders: he must get in among the enemy lines and harass them all night long so that they would be in no condition to launch another attack at dawn. As the last traces of daylight faded from the sky he gathered his men together and told them what they had to do. He chatted and joked as he went from man to man, although he knew that their chances of returning safely were almost non-existent. He was nineteen years old ..."

Nzekwe stopped reading and let the paper flutter from his hand to the ground. "I wish it had been like that," he said. "No matter how terrible, I wish it had been like that. That's how it should be, cardboard people living in clichés. That would remove the smallness and the fear ..."

"What was it like?"

"I'll tell you. I'll tell you how it really was. It was a hymn to futility, a glorious sounding blare of nothingness. The Federals came in along the road using their machine guns like hoses and saturating the bush on either side of it with high velocity bullets. The Biafran soldiers, a crowd of frightened boys, heard them coming and they threw down their guns and ran. They discarded their uniforms and ran naked into the bush, and the villagers watched them go. It still took the Federals two more hours to gather up enough courage to venture into the town. When they did arrive they were quite courteous, but that night they got drunk and they shot some of the people who had stayed behind. They didn't shoot them because they hated them, or because they represented any danger. They felt good, so they fired off their guns, and when the people ran, they shot them out of pure high spirits."

Painter said something indistinctly, but Nzekwe paid no attention to him. "It had no meaning," he went on. "I sat quietly in one of the houses and no one bothered to ask me who I was. I walked about after the shooting stopped, and a girl that I met offered herself to me. I had a conversation with an old man who told me proudly that he was a Christian and that he would not be afraid to die. When morning came the Federals retreated and soon afterwards the Biafran soldiers came back again. It was almost as if they had never been away."

It was beginning to get dark in the room and when Painter suddenly slid off his chair and fell on the floor Nzekwe had to hunt about before he could find him. When he did find him, he fell over him, and they both lay on the ground and giggled. Painter turned over on his back and said in a surprisingly sober voice, "It's better the way you wrote it, it merely made my hair stand on end." He giggled again and said, "I see two pale disembodied ghosts dancing across the face of the moon. I see them peering in through lighted windows. I see spectral shapes and white-faced negroes, and gaping wounds that refuse to bleed. I hear distant laughter and the sound of marching feet, and I'm hiding in tall grass while someone sets fire to it, but I feel no heat. I'm tied between two horses, one white, one black, while they gallop off in different directions. I'm an offering to the Ju-ju, I'm a shade of Christmas past, I'm a pain in the neck ..." He rolled over against Nzekwe and lay against his body, but Nzekwe had stopped laughing and was silent. Painter went on, "I'm an Archbishop of the Church and a master politician. I can form unlimited possibilities to fit an infinity of theories, I can sing a song of sixpence and shit a herd of cows. I'm blind during the day and can see nothing at night, and when bells toll I weep because I cannot hear them."

Nzekwe stirred. He said, "Mutual masturbation might be a fitting ending to the night. I haven't performed since I was a child, with my brother who is now a cook in Port Harcourt. All of my family, and my compound brothers and sisters, have worked in order to educate me. They boast about me, and show me off proudly when I visit them."

"You should be grateful," Painter said. "They've made you what you are." He got up on his hands and knees and leaned over Nzekwe. "You should perform for them at least twice a year, and more often if they demand it. You owe it to them, it's their right." He laughed and began to crawl about until he found the door. He stood up shakily and staggered down the hallway, and when he got outside he turned round once and then sat down on the running board of his car.

70

The sun had set and the air had become chilly, and after a time Painter's head began to clear. The people in the compound were cooking their evening meals over small smoking fires, the women kneading the kassava into a white pulp, while the children poked their fingers into tomato purée and licked at the red blood-like substance. The various odours of an African night hung sharp and suffocating in the windless air: the smell of people living too closely together, the effluvia from open drains and waterless toilets. This blanket of foulness made Painter imagine himself rising into the air to escape from it, to sail away peacefully over the trees and villages, still in a sitting position, and to come down again into some other place, clean and warm and brightly lit. He got up and climbed onto the roof of his Volkswagen and began to jump up and down until he had made a huge dent in the roof of the car. The people stopped and watched him impassively, and soon he lost his balance and fell onto the bonnet, from where he slid slowly to the ground.

When he had got his breath back he went into the house. Nzekwe was pissing carefully and ceremoniously onto the ruined mattress and Painter went and joined him. Having thus relieved their bladders, they went back outside, got into the car and drove down into the town.

9

The Volkswagen rocked and swayed over the rain-eroded ruts in the road, up and over hills and furrows like a ship in a storm. The headlights danced crazily, now poking fingers into the sky, then scraping away the comforting darkness from the faces of people who blinked out of doorways and from under flimsy palm-thatched shelters. A spidery pi-dog who had somehow managed to escape the depredations of hungry children cringed away from the spotlighting brightness, yet moved along beside them as if reluctant to part with human company. Nzekwe sat forward in his seat, and the green dashboard light fell across his face and shirtfront leaving a shadow in between which made him look as if his throat had been cut. Painter remembered the many times he and O'Rourke had driven through these same streets at this same hour of the night, O'Rourke urging him on to drive faster, and waving his anxious silver nitrate-spotted hands about in a semaphore of drunken excitement. He remembered how once when they had a flat tyre O'Rourke had disappeared, and when he went searching for him Painter had found him sitting eating pineapple with a little gummy old man who had known no English but who had nodded his head and repeated "Na" over and over again as if he was telling his beads. Once they had found a body in the road, a body like a tattered foetus, with no head and with the right hand missing, and when they had reported it to the police the sergeant had looked uneasily at the walls of his office, and at the flickering Aladdin lamp, and had told them that he would see about it. But the next morning, when they were returning to Ogundizzy, the body had still been lying in the same position, with the people on their way to market carefully stepping over it, ignoring it and chattering away as if it were not there at all.

Painter glanced at Ben Nzekwe. He said, "Tell me more about Pius Osu and his one-man war. Did he win any more medals?"

"There's nothing more to tell," Nzekwe said. "He was a child. He was not afraid, so he stayed and was killed. He's already forgotten."

"You haven't forgotten him."

"Haven't I? I cannot remember his face, what he looked like; I can only recollect his enthusiasm and how quickly it was snuffed out. Was it Shaw who said that youth is too precious to be given to the young?"

"What would you have had him do, run away with the rest?"

Nzekwe shrugged. He said, "It's the old men and the very young who want this war. The old men are bored, the young men are full with their sense of destiny. I wish I had the courage to run away."

"We're very much alike, Ben. I ..."

"We are not very much alike. In our equivocation, perhaps, but in our situation, no. I am a Biafran, I must decide. You have no need to involve yourself."

"Yes I have."

"I'm sorry, perhaps I should rephrase that. You may have a need, but I have a duty."

"Duty is a cold word, it echoes no passion."

"But like thought, it is rational. I am an intelligent, educated blackman, with my shopping bag of knowledge secure beneath my arm. But my ideas are not even thought out in my own tongue, they are not basic to my situation. When I hear the old shout of Ibo Kwennwu it passes over me like the wind. I have lost something, part of myself ..."

Painter braked suddenly as a line of men ran out in front of the car carrying buckets on their heads like chimney pots. They were the nightsoil workers hurrying to beat the dawn. They carried about with them a smell of corruption.

"I don't know what to say," Painter said. He sat with his hands on the wheel. "Perhaps we should go back."

"Back, back to where? We cannot go back. Back is nothing. We'll press on. I need a drink, I need to sleep with a woman. I cannot even remember what day it is."

"It's Christmas Eve," Painter said. He restarted the engine and turned into a narrow side street. "It's five minutes past twelve, and if we don't hurry the star may have winked out."

They turned through a number of other streets, all equally as deserted as the one that they had been on, and finally they drew up at the entrance to the Paradise Hotel. A dim light was burning over the wrought-iron gate, and an old man wearing a skullcap dozed in a chair just inside the entrance. He was Eusebius, the nightwatch, and while Painter left the engine running, Nzekwe got out and rattled the gate.

The old man jerked awake and reached for a machete which leaned against the wall near him. When he saw who it was he relaxed, took a large red handkerchief out of his pocket, removed his cap and rubbed his bald head. Nzekwe said something to him in Ibo, but when he answered it was in English: "Nobody be for this place. All gone away for Aba side." He made no move to get up off his chair.

Painter got out of the car and climbed up on the gate until he could see inside the hotel. He saw a number of people sitting around a table, and he could hear the clink of glasses and the sound of muted conversation. Suddenly he was seized with an unreasoning anger, and he got down and sat in again behind the wheel of the Volkswagen. He

74

switched on the engine and the lights and he backed the car away from the gate. Then he put it into first gear, revved up the engine and drove straight at the front of the building. The car smashed into the gate, which burst open, sweeping the old man and his chair aside, and the Volkswagen went on into the open courtyard and ended up with its front bumper against the opposite wall.

The crash had barely subsided when Eusebius came out of the darkness, minus his skullcap, and brandishing his old rusty machete like a sword of retribution. He brought the machete down on the bonnet of the car as if he was blaming it, and not Painter, for the attack on his position. He continued to pound on the car until Nzekwe came up behind him and took the machete from his gasp.

The people at the other table had looked around when the car had hit the gate and now one of them left the group and came over to them. He was the owner, a short, very black man whose name was Cardu. He looked like a sucked prune. After surveying the car and the smashed gate for a moment he turned to Nzekwe and said, "You go ruin my doorway proper. Why you do that now?"

No one answered him, but Painter suddenly opened the door of the car and got out and sat at one of the tables. Nzekwe released the nightwatch who immediately began to hunt about frantically on the ground for something. Painter, Nzekwe and the owner of the hotel gazed at him, and they all seemed a little disappointed when he merely retrieved his cap and put it on.

"I go for police," Eusebius said defiantly to Cardu. "You no go stop me, I be insulted too much."

He turned away and marched out around the car, his back stiff and straight and his baggy trousers flapping around his bare ankles like a scarecrow's rags on a windy day.

Nzekwe joined Painter at the table and after a moment

Cardu shrugged his shoulders and said, "You want beer?"

Painter nodded without looking at him. Nzekwe began to beat slowly on the table with the flats of his hands and soon two of the girls at the other table got up and came over to them. One of them was a fat whore named Alice, and the other was the girl from the Rivers whom Painter had slept with during the Wet Season. She looked at him now but he ignored her and pulled Alice down onto his lap. Nzekwe produced a bottle of wine and offered it to the other girl, but when she reached for it he took it back and drank from it himself.

"A pretty girl is like a melody," Painter half sang, and he joggled Alice up and down on his knee. He closed one eye and looked up at the girl from the Rivers. She smiled hesitantly at him, but as soon as she did he closed both eyes and leaned back in his chair. Nzekwe put down the wine bottle and looked from Painter to the girl, and then he got up and took her with him inside the hotel building.

Cardu came back with the beer, but Painter ignored it and drank the wine instead. Alice called him "My man", drawing out the second word until it sounded like the bleating of a sheep, and tried to get him to put his hand under her skirt. After a time she went away looking for more beer and came back to excitedly pull Painter over to where a chink of light showed through a partly covered window. Painter put his eye to the gap and in the stark white light of the room within he saw Nzekwe lying on a bed on top of the girl from the Rivers. The girl's face was turned towards him and she seemed to be gazing straight into his eyes.

He jerked away from the scene and looked at Alice, who was grinning and nodding lecherously at him, and he raised his hand and struck her once, twice, three times across the face.

There was a commotion outside and the owner came in and said something to Alice. She turned her tear-stained face towards Painter, but he pushed her aside and went back down to the entrance. Two uniformed constables and a sergeant were standing surveying his Volkswagen. Eusebius was with them and he looked triumphantly at Painter and said something to the sergeant in Ibo. He did not reply, but stood silently looking from the car to the gate, until Painter finally said, "It's not badly damaged. It needs a new lock ..."

Immediately Eusebius began to talk excitedly again, but no one paid any attention to him. The sergeant was in his forties, a heavy-set man with grizzled hair and a growth of some kind on his left cheek. He grinned at Painter, and Painter grinned back at him; they were like old friends who had not met for a long time and were now preparing to embrace.

The sergeant, still smiling at Painter, spoke to one of his constables, and the young policeman came over and handed him his truncheon. The sergeant gently lifted the nightwatch's cap and Painter flinched as the truncheon bounced on the old bald pate. "Credo in unum deum," the sergeant said, and he replaced the cap.

Eusebius blinked, but his mouth remained open revealing blackened gums and a surprisingly pink tongue. The sergeant looked at him for the first time and said, "Old man, the next time you come to me with complaint, show money first. Now go away and do not trouble me or this man again."

Once again everyone stared at the nightwatch, Painter and the sergeant, Alice from the doorway of the hotel, the people at the other table, and under the weight of all that scrutiny, he turned and shuffled away into the darkness.

The sergeant handed back the truncheon and extended his hand to Painter. "My name is Ukeji," he said. "Perhaps I have been of service?"

Painter nodded and shook the proffered hand. They sat down and Cardu came out to them with glasses and two bottles of flat Golden Guinea beer. He looked at the money which Painter had placed on the table, but Sergeant Ukeji picked it up and put it in the pocket of his tunic. Painter paid for the beer and told Cardu to bring some for the constables as well.

The sergeant filled his glass and drank off the beer in one draught. As he slowly refilled the glass he said, "The old man – he is mad. What did he expect to gain?"

Painter shrugged his shoulders and said nothing. He stared over the sergeant's head at the constables, who were sitting with their backs against the Volkswagen and nodding off to sleep.

"I cannot understand these people," the sergeant went on as if he were talking about some race foreign to him. "They do not know their place. One would think that someone as old as he would be able to control himself." He sounded genuinely puzzled.

Painter looked at him and his face darkened as if he were becoming angry, but then he sighed and laid his hands flat on the table. He said, "He is stubborn. And stupid. It doesn't matter." As if it explained everything he said, "Tomorrow it will be Christmas Day. Peace on earth, good will to men. Perhaps it will be a time of renewal?"

"Yes," the sergeant agreed, but he did not seem very interested. He looked meaningfully at his empty bottle and glass and when Painter did not respond he called Cardu over himself.

The beer arrived and the sergeant started to talk about the old days when the British were in control, and of how good they were. Painter stared at the black face opposite him, and watched the mouth opening and closing, but he had stopped listening to the words. His head was dizzy and he wished that the sergeant would cease talking and would go away. He felt that there was something that he had to do, but he could not remember what it was, and the more he searched his mind the more it escaped him. He stood up but then sat down again and leaned his head on the table. The sergeant reached over and slapped him on the shoulder and he straightened up, but soon his head began to nod again. He must have dozed for a time for, when he suddenly awoke again with a jerk, the sergeant was gone. Nothing remained of him but the residue of froth in his glass and one brass button that had fallen from his tunic onto the table.

Painter stood up shakily and went outside. The air was close and heavy and smelled of rotting vegetation and dusty earth. A few stars glinted impersonally through a frieze of dirty cloud, and the whine of a mosquito only served to accentuate the torpidity of the night. Painter walked a short distance out into the street, but then he turned and went back inside the hotel. He felt very drunk, and an attack of hiccups made his body rattle and shake like a marionette's. He opened various doors, but he could find no one to sleep with, and when he shouted only the echoes of his voice answered him. He felt as if he were standing at one end of a long passageway which had many turnings and dark entrance ways, and away in the distance, hanging forlornly in space, was the face of Ben Nzekwe. A hard white light shone on it and the lips were moving, and they repeated one word, over and over again, but Painter could not make out what that word was. He tried to run towards the bearded face, but as soon as he got close to it a transformation took place, and he beheld the girl from the Rivers, with her legs wide apart and a smile of tumescent invitation on her young face. He turned and twisted, trying one branching passageway after another, but each time he ended up as far away from that hanging face as before. And the word kept floating towards him, at one moment whispered so quietly that he could hear it only as a soft susurration, then in the next moment it boomed about his ears like a huge rushing wind in which there was no sound, only motion. The ground beneath his feet began to rock, and the walls to shake, and he heard a voice cry out, and it was his own, but then a door opened and the fat whore, Alice, held him in her arms. He got sick while she held his head and crooned "My man" at him, and as the beer flowed out of him so did the dizziness, until he was lying across a bed, his mouth opening and closing, retching and crying down into a white chamberpot full of vomit.

He slept for a while, cradled in Alice's arms, and when he awoke a grey light was filtering into the room and it had become very cold. Alice held him while he struggled, then she let him go and he rolled over and fell off the bed. He got to his knees and then to his feet, and with the girl guiding him he went out onto the balcony. The town and the land stretching away beyond it were flat and characterless; the grey light diffused and absorbed shape and texture so that for a moment Painter felt as if he were looking out over some barren planet where no man had set foot before. But even as he watched the sun began to nudge the long banks of purple cloud in the east, and a cirrus of peach and coral light almost imperceptibly stippled the sky overhead. There were no sounds, and the stone of the balcony rail was cold to the touch, but the air smelled clean and renewed, and for a fleeting moment Painter felt a sense of something like desolation, as if he had lost a precious object which until that moment he had never known he had owned.

10

The sun was higher now: it was a misanthropic burning ball in the sky, and there were hammers in Painter's head which caused bright shining streaks of pain to lance his skull each time he moved. He stood outside the Paradise Hotel, one hand shading his eyes, and gazed at what remained of his Volkswagen. It had been neatly placed on four supports, and it needed them, for the wheels had been removed.

He opened the door and looked under the back seat, but there was only a gaping hole where the battery should have been. He let the seat fall back into place and leaned across it until his glasses steamed up from the heat and the world tilted slightly to the left, or perhaps it was to the right, he did not really care. He felt at least one hundred years old. He smelled of beer and stale vomit, and his newly grown beard was like a sentient thing: it crept and crawled about his face and itched so badly that he would have liked to have torn it out in tufts.

He got back out of the car and leaned against the roof, but when he put his arm against the metal it burned him and he jerked away from it. "God damn and blast you," he muttered, and he turned away and began to walk down the street. He had gone only a little way when he discovered that one of his shoes was missing.

A thin man on a bicycle passed by and saluted him – "Good morning, Fada" – but Painter did not raise his head. He walked across a strip of dusty road and into the motor park, where one ancient Mammy Wagon stood parked under a tarpaulin and a row of decrepit bicycles leaned against one another awaiting owners who would probably never come to claim them. A small naked boy with an umbilical hernia like a second penis came out of a shed and stared about him. He began to suck his thumb. Painter tried to grin at him, and his face felt as if it were cracking open.

The child turned and went back into the shed, and without thinking about it Painter followed him inside. It was so dark that at first he could see nothing, but as his eyes grew accustomed to the gloom he perceived an old woman lying on a mat in one corner. He was about to say something, a word of greeting, when he saw that her eyes were sightless and staring, and the one arm raised in the air was motionless and stiff as if she had been trying to point something out to the child and had died before the act was completed. Painter tried to draw the child back outside, but he only stood and gazed at the woman on the floor, and with a shock Painter realised that she was probably his mother. Although she appeared to be very old, she was possibly only in her twenties; starvation and hardship had conspired together to make her old while she was still young.

Painter went outside and across the road to where Ben Nzekwe had appeared and was sitting against the wall of the hotel on a hard chair. He was wearing a faded straw hat with an artificial flower in the crown and his feet were bare.

"There's a dead woman over there," Painter said, pointing at the shed. For some reason he remembered an old joke that ended – "That's no lady, that's my wife" – and he suddenly felt like giggling. Nzekwe continued staring in front of him and made no sign that he had heard him.

Painter squatted down on his heels in the dust and closed his eyes tightly. "Did you hear what I said?" he asked. Nzekwe tilted the brim of the hat over his forehead. "I heard you," he said.

"Well?"

"There are dead women everywhere, and dead men, and dead children. What's one dead woman among so many?"

Painter opened his eyes and moved, still squatting, into the shade of the wall. The hard white glare of sunlight in the road seemed like a barrier between him and the other side. He said, "There's a child. I tried to bring him out but he refused to come."

Nzekwe got up and went across the road. The shimmering waves of heat made him appear to float rather than walk. When he came back he was carrying the child. He sat down again on the chair and placed the little boy on his lap. After a time the child began to suck his thumb and to make small nondescript sounds like a bird fluttering about in a bush.

"What will you do with him?" Painter said.

"Perhaps I'll sit here with him until we both wither up and blow away in the wind."

"He may be hungry."

"So?"

Nzekwe's eyes were hidden by the brim of the hat. He made no effort to comfort the child in any way, he merely held him loosely on his lap as one might hold a toy doll.

"What would you do for him?" he asked Painter. "Do you feel pity for him? His mother is dead, he may well be all alone in the world. Would you say that his chances of survival are good?" He stood up and let the child swing downwards. Holding him about the ankles in one hand he said, "Would I not be doing him a service if I were to smash his head against this wall? If he's baptised he'll go straight to heaven. Your priests will tell you that. Otherwise we can do nothing for him, neither you nor I. It only seems as if we can. We can feed him, and we can pat his little head and make him feel safe and secure and maybe even cause him to smile. And for what? So that tomorrow he can suffer the same all over again, and again the day after. Who will comfort him then, and who will comfort all the others? Here, take him," he shoved the child at Painter – "Tell him that everything is all right, that he'll never be sad or cold or hungry again. Tell him that his mother is young and beautiful and alive, and that when night descends she'll be there in the darkness to reassure him and to whisper love words in his ear. Tell him that he's an Ibo, but more than that, tell him that he's a Biafran. Tell him that his agony is part payment for a dream of freedom which will never be realised, and tell him that it is all worthwhile. I cannot."

Painter huddled closer into the shade of the wall and wrapped his hands around his knees. He began to rock backwards and forwards. "We are rational, sane people," he said. "In a few hours time we will all go to Mass. All over the world people will go to Mass, or to some such service, and they'll rejoice in that other dream of the first Christmas. Such pious aspirations will bloom in the minds of so many people, in the minds of princes and kings, of politicians and soldiers, of ordinary good people. The guns will stop and they'll be replaced by the joyous ringing of bells. Can such beauty beget madness? Famine and slaughter, conquest and death, they are an illusion also, they are bred of bad dreams. Because we care. Don't we care?"

Nzekwe did not answer. He took the straw hat off his head and placed it on the shrivelled head of the child, who had become quiescent again. Then he looked at Painter. He said, "Does it really touch you? Are you here because you want to play a part? Are you not just an observer? What can you do?"

"The Bishop asked me that also," Painter said. He stared out into the sunlight. "I can do nothing, but I'm no different from anyone else except possibly the priests. It's an act of defiance ..."

"Defiance? Who are you defying?"

"Myself."

"I don't understand."

Painter sighed. He said, "Ben, I want you to understand. You, more than anyone. But I can't put it into words. Last night I was drunk, and after the sergeant had gone I imagined I saw you. You called me a parasite, over and over you said it, and I wanted to explain to you that you were wrong. I may appear to be drifting along without feeling anything, but that's my way. I don't enjoy watching people suffer, seeing the land devastated ... I'm not indifferent to the plight of the people."

"I don't believe you." Nzekwe cradled the child in his arms and looked into Painter's face. "You're using the situation here for your own purposes. Most people lead dull and frustrated lives. Boredom and frustration, rather than hatred or envy, are more often the causes of unreasonable acts. There is no such thing as a truly good or altruistic person. St Thomas and St Augustine both sought quite seriously to define the concept of a just war. You spoke of parasites. Peace carries about its own parasite, because peace is really a state of reconciliation after a period of war and strife. There cannot be one without the other."

"Then what does man aspire to?"

Suddenly Nzekwe grinned. "Man aspires to be like the God that made him," he said. "And as I see Him, when he created man, God was bored."

"A bored God ..."

"God is not black or white. He is grey. Grey for disinterest. Love and hatred, grief and jealousy, spite and greed, these are transitory; they come and they go. But boredom is always present in the mind of man. It never goes away. It never even becomes dormant."

"Do you really believe that?"

"No, I don't. I'm only saying these things because I want to talk." Nzekwe stopped and leaned his chin on the crown

85

of the hat on the child's head. Sweat dripped off his face and hung on the edges of his beard like dew. He said, "I sit here and I speak to you, and all the while there is a tiny voice somewhere in my head and it is screaming. I listen to it and it tells me nothing. I wait for it to become louder and it never does. It is always there, just on the edge of consciousness, and it makes me uneasy rather than mad." He paused, then he added as if in answer to a question, "I cannot help you."

"Help!" Painter stood up and thrust his face at Nzekwe. "I don't need any help. I'm my own man. I go my own way and I'm never tired of my company. I can live in my mind quite happily. I'm a free spirit ..."

"Can you feel compassion?"

"Yes, I can."

"For others as well as for yourself?"

"Yes."

Nzekwe turned away. He said over his shoulder, "I envy you. You are a man among men. When you have a moment you must teach me compassion. It will purge me of so much." He went inside the hotel, and the hard line of shadow, which had moved closer to the wall, left Painter standing once more in the bright glare of the sun. He stood with his mouth open, as if he were about to say something further, but then he turned away and walked once more across the road towards the motor park. Inside the hotel a child began to wail, and in the streets only the heat waves moved and shimmered in the stillness.

11

Anne Siena walked slowly down the hill towards the town. The moon was up and the night was almost as bright as day. As she walked, the silent people moved aside and then fell in behind her as if they expected her to lead them somewhere. She passed the deserted buildings of the girls' school; she came to the Welfare Hotel, and the three or four girls on the verandah smiled at her until she nervously looked away from them; and when she came to the church, the young soldiers standing at the door shoved people roughly away to allow her in.

The church was huge and cold and unfinished. It had been started by Father Manton's predecessor, who had done some years as an engineering student before he had entered the Order as a late vocation, and it bore witness to the fact that the man had made the correct decision in giving up his idea of becoming an engineer. Father Manton had been defeated by its size, and after many months it was still roofless, cement blocks formed the seating, and grass grew everywhere except in front of the altar.

The girl ignored the line of prie-dieus, which had been set up at the front of the church for herself, the nuns and Painter, and she went and sat on a rough cement block among the native women. She felt tired, and she wished that she had a support for her back. She gazed about her at the women, many of whom were breast-feeding their babies, and the pungent smell of sweat and urine almost made her gag. She was sorry now that she had not sat with the nuns.

For the women, this Mass in the middle of the night was a gala occasion, an opportunity for them to be seen in their best Mammy clothes, a time for gossip and excited chattering, while their men sat morose and uncomfortable in their ill-fitting Western suits in their segregated portion of the church. Every night of the year but this night, the women of Ogundizzy were asleep by seven o'clock, to arise at daybreak to another round of work and back-breaking labour. They hoed the fields, carried water, haggled in the market place, and satisfied their husbands, and they aged prematurely like trees in an early autumn. It was the Ibo custom that females too should be circumcised, so that the sexual act became for the women merely the promise of another childbirth, and they did bear innumerable children, many of them by Caesarean section because their hips and pelves had been damaged by years of carrying heavy loads on their heads. In time, through feeding the children, their breasts became like razor strops, their faces rough and coarsened by wind and rain took on the appearances of well-travelled roads, and they often just faded away rather than died. Yet they accepted their lot, loved their children fiercely, and tolerated their husbands, with a selflessness that was yet totally subjective, for their sense of identity was completely dependent on their usefulness to their men and the amount of love that they bestowed upon their children.

Anne Siena remembered a sentence from the past – "The idea of total commitment can give one a real sense of personal significance" – and it surprised her that she had to search her mind for a moment before she could recollect who had said it. It had been Father Quale of course, her friend, counsellor and chaplain in the convent, and most probably, she supposed, it had formed the cornerstone of her decision to come to Africa.

She looked about her again, now almost fondly, at the women. Certainly their enthusiastic reception of the

Christian ethic was easily understood; they would need no priest to explain to them the intricacies of St Paul's words: "Love bears all things, believes all things, hopes all things, endures all things," and again: "So faith, hope, love abide, all three; but the greatest of these is love." How she could have used a little of their patient resignation, the girl thought. She saw herself as she had been when she had left the convent: depressed at the thought that God had turned his back on her, had spurned her weak and tentative offer. And yet, as she now also recalled, she had felt, however guiltily, a great sense of release. She had wanted to embrace people, to sing and to dance and to thumb her nose at the painted statues of the saints in the churches.

But she soon realised that, like the Establishment in general, the Church, too, was loath to give up its victims. She was only out on parole, and Father Quale was to be her parole officer. She could see him again now just as clearly as if he had been standing in front of her: his neat young face and figure, the black clothes suiting his becoming pallor – he had looked more like one of those antiseptic male models one sees in a glossy magazine than a priest. Yet he had been so kind and so comforting, so safe ... When he had mentioned Africa she had been immediately eager to go; it was the substitute sacrifice she was looking for. She had gladly accepted the conditions demanded, including the three-year vow of chastity; her mind was encompassed in a spiritual maze and her evanescent flirtation with God transcended the yearnings of the flesh.

She had been able to uproot her life from the small Mid-Western town where she had lived all of her life, without causing any upheavals to either herself or the town. She had simply packed some suitcases, wept dispassionately with her father over her mother's grave, and left. It had been as simple as that.

For a time Africa had been everything she had hoped it

would be. Her training as a postulant had enabled her to give, and to keep on giving, and it did not matter if the people were grateful or not. She had been sent to a small hospital run by an order of Irish nuns. It was situated in the bush near Na'wadi: a neat, well-kept compound, with one-storeyed sturdy wards, each one separate from the other but connected by covered-in cement walks, a small air-conditioned operating theatre, and carefully tended beds of flowers everywhere like warnings to the voracious bush not to attempt to claim back its own. She had been happy there, keeping the accounts and doing the office work and haggling by letter with various charitable organisations all over the world. The nuns had taken a little time to accept her brash American voice and manner and they had given her a house at the opposite end of the compound from the convent, but she ate with them, worked alongside them, prayed with them, and in time, perhaps also like them, convinced herself she was content. The priests invited her to their houses, the younger ones taking small liberties like looking at her legs when they thought she was not paying any attention to them, being childishly daring in their conversations, but again, like children, they were easily distracted.

She had arrived in Nigeria during the Wet Season, and in the middle of the following Dry Season she had been transferred to Ogundizzy Hospital. Igor had given a party to welcome her and it was at this party that she had met Painter for the first time. He had been drunk, but unlike his friend O'Rourke, who had also been there, he had been morose and uncommunicative. Yet as the night wore on she had become grateful for Painter's presence, for amidst her uncertainty in her new surroundings and what with O'Rourke's rough attempts to frighten her with talk of snakes and thiefmen, Painter's tired smile and sincere inattention had strangely comforted her.

During the weeks that followed O'Rourke had persisted in his loud courtship, but he was so obvious and so like the priests in his contentment with a smile or a sisterly kiss that he had been easy to handle. Painter seldom called on her and when he did, he came to talk. He never spoke of needing anything, rather he spoke with enthusiasm of his work and of his hopes for his students, but after a time she began to sense that his idealism was slightly frayed about the edges. It was never anything that he said, but she felt a restlessness in him, he seemed to lack a basic sense of urgency, as if he were waiting for something to happen, something outside himself which would give an impetus and a deeper meaning to who he was and to what he was doing. She began to worry about him and to look forward to his visits, and it was only when he began to talk about wanting her that she realised that he had mistaken her liking for him for something else. She had convinced herself that she wanted to be his friend, she had been able to talk so easily to him, and now he was spoiling it by wanting to sleep with her. Yet there were times when she knew that she would have given in to him – in spite of her vow of celibacy and in spite of Father Quale's trust in her – but somehow Painter had talked on and on, and the moments had been lost. It was a simple situation, but a human one, and because neither of them had availed of the many opportunities which had occurred to resolve it, the basic situation had become complicated, and tension and unease had set in where formerly there had been companionship and not a little laughter. The girl sighed as she remembered how happy she had been: it was unfair that something which had almost become a reality should have been dissipated by such emotive stupidity.

She gazed about her at the mass of rustling humanity, and in the dim light shed by the storm lanterns and the flickering candles the people were indistinguishable one

91

from another. Only their eyes shone, but they were sightless and staring like the eyes of drowned people. The girl looked up at the altar and, in the wavering light, the figure on the cross seemed to move, and she wondered if, in fact, God was really present in that dank and starlit place. The nuns' backs were towards her, and they appeared stiff and disapproving and completely out of her reach. She wished with all her heart that Painter would come and sit beside her and perhaps take her hand, but when she tried to conjure up his face it was obliterated by other faces, all too familiar, but not his. "Please God," she whispered. "Please God ...", but she could think of nothing further to say, for she was not sure what she was about to ask for. As Father Manton came out on the altar, and as a smell of incense began slowly to pervade the darkened church, the people knelt, and the girl also bent forward in the cold grass and joined in the responses, and their voices rose and fell reverently as the first Christmas Mass began.

12

"Good afternoon, Sah."

Painter groaned and raised his head. He stared blearily at the two little naked boys who were standing, side by side, up close against his bedroom window. He waved them away and turned over on his back and gazed through the mosquito net at the lizards scuttling across the ceiling. It suddenly came to him that, today being Christmas Day, there should be some presents at the foot of his bed. He looked, but there was nothing except a dirty stain where his feet had soiled the sheet.

He groaned again and slid out under the net, and stood weaving gently in the muggy air. Waves of nausea flowed through him and the heat flowed up through the soles of his feet and burst like a minor explosion somewhere near the top of his head. He hitched up the pants of his pyjamas and went out into the living room and through the open front door. He stood in the shadow cast by the overhang of the roof and squinted into the brilliant light. From his house he could look down over the countryside for many miles, but there was nothing to see, for the land was nondescript and tattered like refuse at the bottom of a garden. The lake was the only compromise made by nature, but now in the late afternoon light it was only a glitter of coruscation, hurtful to the eyes.

With paralytic strides he made his way around the house, the hard laterite pathway burning the soles of his bare feet, and stood looking at the little boys, who were

93

washing his clothes, pounding them between two stones and chattering like monkeys as they worked.

"Where's Jude?" Painter said.

The boys stopped and gazed at him, the water silvering down off their satiny skin, and they both shrugged in unison as if they operated on strings.

The smaller of them giggled and said, "Jude, he be gone for market. He say he be back by six o'clock." He looked at his companion as if for confirmation.

Painter rubbed his eyes, then he said, "Who you be now?"

"We be brothers of Jude," the smaller one again said.

"Same father, same mother?"

"We be compound brothers. No same father, same mother."

They were almost identical in size, shape and colour, both of them about nine years old, and their teeth glinted in the sun as they grinned at Painter.

"What are your names?" he asked them.

They both giggled this time as the smaller one said, "I be Jesus Christ Osuiji and he be Mercedes Benz Osuiji. We be training to be cooks proper," he added, as Painter gazed in astonishment from one to the other of them.

"A true example of Christian materialism," he said. "I'm glad to know you. Just carry on, you can't possibly go wrong."

He went back inside the house. The bedroom smelled of sweat and soiled clothes, and the sight of the crumpled sheets on the bed made Painter feel sick again. He stripped off his pyjamas and wrapped a towel around his waist and, taking up a bar of soap and his shorts, he went back out into the quivering air. He walked down the narrow mango-strewn pathway that ran along by the side of Mr Bristol's garden, a garden now overgrown and unkempt and full of anthills like crumbling clay monuments. In the past Painter

94

had often helped old Bristol to excavate those hills, both of them taking turns to dig down into the earth until they uncovered the queen, a membraned monstrosity like the inside of a giant golf ball. Now the ants had the garden to themselves.

The pathway ended at the beginning of the hill which led down to the stream. The hill was badly fissured by erosion, huge cavities fell away abruptly on either side, but about halfway down it curved sharply and the lower slope straightened out and became more gradual. At the bottom there was a small stone bridge, and below this bridge the river widened and became a sliding current of dappled water. Hibiscus grew there, Flame of the Forest flared in the undergrowth, and there was a cool odour of fern and damp moss.

A number of women knelt in the shallow water beside the bridge washing kassava. They were all curiously similar in appearance, old age and hard work having combined to make them so. Flat-chested and toothless, with gaily coloured scarves wrapped around their heads, they resembled a line of washing flapping and cracking in the wind. They could hardly contain their merriment when Painter dropped his towel and dived into the swirling water.

He washed himself in the water above the women, the soap suds whirling away beneath the bridge, and when he had finished he lit a cigarette and let himself float about slowly in the current. The two little boys arrived and began to sport about, diving deep down into the stream with hardly a splash, and coming up beside him grinning like waterhens. He half expected them to be holding fish between their teeth.

It was very peaceful, and Painter could feel the tiredness easing out of his body and out of his mind like snow melting in the sun. He began to sing, a Christmas song to which he could just about put the words, and the women joined in with some songs of their own. Startled by the sound of the singing voices, two stately egrets rose in the air like disapproving spinster aunts, and then settled again soundlessly into the undergrowth. Dragonflies and huge multicoloured butterflies hovered above the surface of the water, and the scent from the large purple flowers growing by the side of the stream lay on the air like incense.

When the sun began to go down behind the tall trees to his left Painter came out of the water, dried himself and put on his shorts. One very withered old woman came over to him and put her hand on his bare shoulders, and she nodded her head at him as if thanking him for something. He nodded his head in return and said, "Ah, Missus, you go flirt with me too much," and she cackled happily as if she understood what he had said.

Painter walked back up the hill and when he got to the bend in the pathway he turned and looked back, but the shadows had begun to lengthen across the water and the women were gathering up their possessions and were preparing to go. The two little boys came up the hill and stood beside him and looked curiously into his face, and when he saw them staring at him he grinned and said, "Some people weep when they are happy. It's something that comes only in very rare moments. It can be a great relief, the ability to weep. Do you understand what I mean?" he asked them, but he knew that they did not, for they were too young and their English was very poor.

13

"I've just received word that all the women are being moved out tomorrow," Anne Siena said.

She was sitting beside Painter on the verandah of his house, and away behind the banks of cloud in the west where the sun had gone down, colour gleamed in the sky like old gold.

"Are you going?" Painter asked.

"I have no choice, the Bishop has ordered it."

"I forgot your vow of obedience."

"There's no need to be unkind. Onitsha is under heavy attack. It will only be a matter of time before it is captured."

Painter lit a cigarette. He drank some beer and watched a breeze stir the fronds of the palm trees beside the house. He did not answer when the girl said, "Have you decided when you are going to leave? This may be one of the last planes out of Port Harcourt." Behind them in the lighted house the two little Osuijis, with scrubbed shining faces and wearing white smocks, moved soundlessly about.

A car came around the turn in the road and its headlights flashed across the verandah so that for a moment the two of them were floodlit, pinned in their chairs by the twin beams of brightness. The car stopped in front of Kappel's deserted house and a drunken female laugh was wafted across to them like a gibe at their own solemnity. "At least Igor still believes in fornication," Painter said, and he glanced at the girl, but she was not to be sidetracked that easily. "O'Rourke has gone," she said, continuing her original train of thought, "Kappel has left. You're the only one remaining, except for the priests."

Painter did not reply, and after a moment he stood up and walked to the edge of the verandah. The girl followed him and leaned against his side, and he put out his hand to her. She stood in the curve of his arm and he put his cheek against her hair and watched a star which had appeared in the blue-black emptiness of the sky, a constant star. He said, "You go out with the other women this week, and I'll follow you on the next available plane."

"There may not be another plane."

"They're building a new airport at Uli. It will be easy to get out from there."

"Why not come now?"

Painter sighed. He felt an old irritation picking at his mind, he wanted to be away from the girl, out of her company. He said gently, "Let's enjoy this last evening. The others will be here soon. We don't want to be sad when they come."

"I don't know why you had to invite them," the girl said. "We should have been alone tonight, together." She did not seem to notice the contradiction in her words.

The Barkers arrived just then, appearing out of the fading light like people who had lost their way and were only stopping for a moment to ask for directions. They were soon followed by Lennox who had come down from the hospital in Odisi. The Barkers were waiting to go out on the plane on the following day and were staying with Father Manton. John Barker was English and his wife, Eileen, was Irish. He was a quiet, pipe smoking man who spoke very little, but his wife made up for his silence by being highly voluble. Lennox was a doctor; he was a short, easily dislikeable man of indeterminate age who had only been shamed into staying by the fact that many of the women had chosen to remain. He too was leaving on the same plane as the others.

They sat on the darkened verandah and smoked and drank beer, and after a time Painter began to feel a maudlin affection for Lennox and the Barkers and an increasing irritation with Anne Siena, who sat silently, a cold accusing figure in the half-light.

"Come on," he said, leaning across and putting his hand on her arm. "Cheer up, it may never happen."

The girl looked at him. "You're disgusting," she said quietly, but fiercely. "A few drinks and you can forget a war, and other people's unhappiness. I mean absolutely nothing to you."

"Yes you do, you're the girl who helped me to preserve my virtue."

The girl drew back in her chair as if he had slapped her. She said faintly into the darkness, "You dirty thing, you don't deserve love."

"I don't desire it either," Painter said, leaning forward. "It makes too many demands."

"You led me to believe ..."

"No, I never led you to believe anything, that was of your own choosing. I merely told you that I wanted you, and I may have used words that you associate with something else. One does that to make it easier ..."

"It doesn't work like that," the girl said miserably. "I've always believed that if you cared for someone hard enough they would in turn begin to care for you."

"I do care for you. I like you. Is that not sufficient reason for two people to go to bed together? I know husbands and wives who hate one another." Painter glanced across at the Barkers and Lennox, but they were studiously ignoring himself and the girl. He leaned back towards Anne Siena, but she twisted away from him and gazed out into the darkness, and he whispered again, "I do care for you."

The girl laughed bitterly. "It's too late," she said. "I might have believed you yesterday."

Father Manton arrived, and brought with him a Father Jones who had been stationed in Enugu. He was a small man with bandy legs and he still retained a spry cheerfulness after thirty years on the coast. His mission had been overrun, and his parishioners scattered, and now, like the others, he was waiting to go home. He talked about the fall of Enugu: "The Federal guns lit up the sky like artificial sunsets. It reminded me of fireworks displays when I was young," and when Anne Siena asked him if he were glad to be going home, he said, "It's funny how one keeps on referring to Ireland as home. Most of my relations are dead, and my friends have grown old or have drifted away. What will I do?"

"Come on, Con," Father Manton said awkwardly, "it's Christmas night. This is no time to be sad."

"Sadness is not something that depends on time or place," John Barker suddenly said. He glanced at his wife. "It's like the poor, it's always with us."

Father Jones stood up and moved out of the circle of light cast by the Aladdin lamp. His voice, as it came out of the darkness, sounded tired and far away. "When I came to Nigeria first," he said, "I met a young chief. He was a good man, but he was a pagan, and he had many wives. I wanted to convert him, and once I had him almost talked into becoming baptised. Then he asked me what would become of his wives when he put them away from him. They wouldn't be able to fend for themselves, and no man would marry them. I told him that God would take care of them, but he did not believe me, and he never did come to be baptised. We grew old together and we remained friends, and I never mentioned his becoming a Christian again. The last time I saw him was two months ago when we were told to evacuate the Enugu area. He was sitting in his house waiting for the Federals to march into his village. He joked with me and said that the soldiers had done what God could

100

not do, for his wives were all gone, and only his first wife, too old and tired like himself to run, was left." He paused, and a wind that smelled of rotting fish, blew up from the direction of the lake. When it seemed as if he had finished he suddenly said, "It doesn't seem to matter to me anymore. The fact that I failed to convert him, I mean. You go down a road and you keep wanting to see around the next bend, and still you long for the familiar way that you've left behind. Perhaps I didn't try hard enough."

When the beer began to run out Painter suggested that they go in to dinner. At first everyone tried earnestly to be cheerful, but the meal was a disaster. It was too hot for eating soup, roast and mashed yam, rubbery chicken and tinned Christmas pudding. Even the champagne, one lone bottle that Painter had saved most carefully, had gone flat. When they had finished they sat around the untidy table and tried to avoid one another's eyes. The beer was finished, there was no one to take upon himself the burden of convincing them that they should enjoy themselves, and the flowers which Jude had so optimistically placed in a bottle on the middle of the table had tiredly wilted.

"We're thrown too much in one another's company, I suppose, to have anything to say," Father Manton said, and it sounded as if he were apologising to someone for their uneasy silence.

The car that had passed earlier in the evening suddenly appeared again, coming from the direction of Kappel's house with a great grinding of gears and flashing of lights. It had almost gone past Painter's driveway when someone seemed to have a change of mind, and it slewed around and came to a stop. There was a muttering of voices, then one of the doors opened and Igor got out and walked up to and into the house. The people inside watched him come, and although no one spoke, there was an almost palpable coming together, an implicit air of concern, as if Igor might

101

prove to be the catalyst which would allow out into the open words and feelings, thoughts and little fears, which so far had lain safely hidden beneath a thin veneer of boredom ad conventionality; and that certain tightening of the features which betokens forced politeness fell over the faces of Painter's guests like masks.

Igor was drunk. He held it well, but it was apparent in the careful way he walked and in the slightly dislocated look of his eyes. He came inside the room and surveyed the people present, gazing carefully at each one as if he wished to preserve their images in his mind for some future date. He was sweating freely and for once he looked his age.

Painter pushed back his chair and stood up. He looked about him but no one gave him any help. He said, "Come and join us," and he showed the palms of his hands as if to let Igor know that he had a choice in the matter.

Igor smiled slowly and almost sadly. He said, "I was not invited to your celebration." He put up his hand and wiped sweat from his forehead, and behind him the lights of the car suddenly winked out as if he had given some signal. He smiled again and said, "You are my friends. Is Christmas not the great Christian feast of friendship?"

Painter grinned at him. "Come on, Igor," he said, "we all know you. You don't know anything about friendship. You brought us here because we were useful to you. Even Father Manton ..."

"Don't say that," Father Manton broke in, but he looked at no one in particular when he said it.

"Why are you all the same colour?" Igor went on, as if no one had spoken. "Could you not have found even one of my countrymen to join with you at this time? Does the message not go out to all men?" His tone of voice took away any criticism from his words, for he spoke slowly and dispassionately like someone whose mind was not tuned to what he was saying.

102

There was a silence in the room, the occupants sitting about like actors who had forgotten their lines, and when Eileen Barker began to cry softly, her sobs echoed like the sound of pebbles dropped into a deep well. Her husband stared helplessly at the rest of them and sucked on his empty pipe, and it was Father Jones who attempted to comfort her.

"I was in Obudu at this time last year," he said. "It reminded me of Scotland with its soft misting rain and green rolling hills. It was very cold at night and there were no mosquito nets. On Christmas Day I went for a walk with an Indian man and his wife who were staying there also. They had been thirty years in Nigeria, and they talked of retiring and of going back to India. They didn't really mean it, of course, it was their Christmas present to themselves. India would have been just as foreign to them as Nigeria." He stopped and idly picked at the greyish tablecloth, then he added, "Why do people always long for something which they know in their heart of hearts doesn't really exist?"

Painter, who was still standing, said, "We substitute a half-remembered moment from the past for the actuality of the present, or the terror of the future. Is it not always so?"

"What are you saying?" Igor said, and his voice had suddenly become harsher and more authoritative. He advanced on the table like a prisoner who had been given a too grievous sentence. "How many times have you visited my house, partaken of my hospitality? Did you not smile, and tell me how grateful you were to me? I have always treated you as equals. I have praised you, and told you of the good you were bestowing upon my country. Yet you now ignore me like a dog who has become diseased. Am I an animal who has no feelings? I am wealthier than you, and I have many sons. By what is a man to be judged? I have done bad things, what man has not? Once I was a small child and I ran about naked, and I had no worries. Now I am almost an old man, and I shall soon be one of the elders

103

of my tribe. What man then will revere me? I have no wisdom, no dignity; they will laugh at me behind my back and call me fool, and there will be nothing anymore of value." He stopped, as if the enormity of his vision had become too much for him, and in the silence Lennox suddenly hiccuped loudly.

Immediately there was a general flurry of small movements: Painter sat down, Eileen Barker yawned nervously, Father Manton almost upset a wine glass, and once more the actors had regained their self-possession and were ready to go on with the play. Igor must also have sensed that he was back on his former footing, for he began to move drunkenly about, and again, as if by signal, the lights of his car flashed on and off.

"Your friends are growing impatient," Painter said. He smiled grimly about him and found Anne Siena watching him intently. She said, "Why are people so unkind to each other?" and she looked at him as if she really thought he could answer her question.

"They're not unkind." He took up his empty glass and looked into it, then he added, "They're indifferent. Don't you see? It's a question of identity," but the girl had ceased to listen to him. She stood up and went outside, and only Igor turned to watch her as she walked out past his car and turned down the hill towards the hospital.

With an abrupt movement Painter put his glass back on the table. "What are we doing?" he said savagely. "We should be enjoying ourselves. We can't do anything about the war. Only Father Manton and Father Jones can help the people. In a year, two years, all of this will be forgotten. The dead will be buried and the living will have forgotten them. It's a farce, the whole bloody thing ..." His voice trailed away, and he stared about him at the others who were looking at him in dismay. "I'm sorry," he said. "I wanted this to be a happy night. We may not see each other again for a long time."

It was Igor who answered him: "Leave these people," he said. "I have a woman in my car. Perhaps you know her?" His drunkenness seemed to have disappeared and he looked his old commanding self again. As Painter lifted his head and looked at him he touched himself on the genitals and grinned almost wickedly. "Perhaps you know her?" he said again, and he bowed at Painter like a pimp soliciting customers.

Painter came around the table and brushed past him. He walked out to the car and opened the door and looked at the woman inside. He stood gazing at her for only a moment, then he slammed the door and began to walk down the road which led to the hospital. Igor called out behind him, but he did not turn or look back, and soon he had gone out of earshot.

The moon had risen and the night had turned into a day where there were only two colours, white and black. The dusty road still retained a trace of the heat of the day, and down by the river a bull-frog croaked hoarsely. When he came to the hospital Painter crossed the gravel path leading to the children's ward. He went up the stone steps and stood inside the door and looked at the two little boys who had been brought in that day. They were suffering from kwashiorkor, their outsized heads and reddish hair showing the telltale signs, and their faces were the faces of old men. Could they be the same two little boys, he wondered, who had woken him up that afternoon as they splashed about in the sun? Was it possible that like butterflies they had been born, had aged and were now about to die, all in the space of one day? He felt a sudden desire to run back across the road and tell them he was sorry, but he knew that it would be a wasted journey. They would die also, or they would survive, and it was Ben Nzekwe's bored God who would decide, not he.

He went outside and leaned against a pillar and listened

to the crickets, and after a time Anne Siena came out and stood looking at him. They did not speak, but when she started for her house he walked along beside her, and when the nightwatch appeared it was Painter who took the key from him and unlocked the door.

In the bedroom the girl undressed slowly. The outside light, shining through the mosquito wire, left squares of shadow across her body, and once she stumbled and almost fell, but Painter made no move to help her. Her breasts were slight, and when she lifted her arms above her head to take off her shirt she looked like a boy. Yet there was a dichotomy about her, for below the waist her hips were wide and her buttocks full and heavy like the buttocks of a Rubins nude. When she was completely naked she leaned against the bed with one hand holding onto the support of the mosquito net, and her hair fell across her face so that Painter could not see her expression. He put his hands on her shoulders and drew her to him, but he could still feel a resistance in her, and this excited him. He twisted his fingers in her hair and pulled her head back and kissed her hard on the mouth. Her lips were open, they were cold and they tasted of tears, but he crushed down on her until she was bent back in the shape of a bow. He put his other hand behind her knees and lifted her onto the bed, and part of the mosquito net fell across the whiteness of her body like a veil.

Painter struggled out of his clothes, a red tide of blood surging behind his eyes, and the intensity of his passion caused his body to shake violently like a ship in a stormy sea. He climbed onto the bed and lay above the girl, supported on the palms of his hands, and the moonlight streamed in through the window and broke along the edges of the pale sheets like liquid silver. He stayed as he was until his arms began to quiver with the effort of holding him up, and as he opened his eyes he saw the girl beneath him, and as he stared at her face, with the strands of her hair lying across it like seawrack, its alabaster whiteness reminded him of the face of a statue one sometimes sees in a church, with its stare of abstract piety forever fixed like the death mask of a saint. When his arms finally gave out he let himself down gently, and they lay quietly, side by side, and he smelled her sweat and sensed the cool dampness of the sheets and felt his desire die like faintly fading music.

After a time the girl turned her head and looked into his face. "Why?" she said. Then after a pause: "It's what you've wanted for a long time. Why have you failed?"

"That's it," Painter said, his voice muffled by the sheet. "It's too much like a sacrifice. There's no emotion, no feeling. It's as if you were lying here with me because you had to. As if only your body were involved," he finished lamely, and from somewhere outside the bull-frog croaked again to emphasise the meaninglessness of his words.

The girl raised her hand and began to stroke his back in a perfunctory manner. "When I was a little girl I wanted to be Judy Garland," she said. "She was in so many happy films. There was a time when her life on the screen was more real to me than my own life. People held hands, and laughed and sang and fell in and out of love so easily. I was born in a big frame house in St Louis, you know. I was the only girl in a family of seven and my brothers all adored me. But my mother died soon after I was born, and my father, although he loved us all, hadn't the personality to communicate that love. It was easy to dream." Again she turned her head and looked at Painter. "Do you not even love me a little?" she asked him.

Painter sighed and turned over on his back and looked at the shifting patterns of shadow move across the ceiling. "Yes, I do," he said truthfully. "I do love you a little." He reached down and took her hand and put it to his lips. "It's so simple really," he said. "It's only the consequences of an act which make for complications. I suppose that's why

107

fairytales are so popular: it's so easy to say, 'And they lived happily after after.' Perhaps, like you, I've spent too much of my life in dreaming. It insulates one against so much. It makes one stand back and watch, rather than act."

He lay for a long time, holding the girl's hand and listening to the rustle of the night outside the open window, and when her even breathing told him that she had fallen asleep, he got out of the bed and began to put on his clothes. He left the room without looking at her again, and walked through the darkened living room and opened the outside door. The old nightwatch jumped up from where he was sitting against the wall, and turned his ravaged face towards him, but he did not look at him either. He moved back across the road and went into his own deserted house, but then he changed his mind and went back outside. He got into the car he had borrowed from Father Manton and drove it savagely down the gravelled drive, and out onto the main road. The headlights jumped about as the car hurtled down the hill, and just at the entrance to the town a group of soldiers was illuminated for an instant like a monument to some god of war.

Painter drove up to the Welfare Hotel and let the headlights of the car shine on the front of the building. He got out and hammered on the door, and the sounds of his blows echoed like drumbeats in the stillness of the night. It was Adolphus himself who finally opened the door, peering out fearfully as if he expected some harbinger of death to greet him. Painter said nothing, but brushed past him and went inside and up the stone stairs.

He began to open various doors, flinging them aside noisily, until Adolphus caught up with him and pulled him back by the arm. "Where is she?" Painter said. "I know she's here. Which room is she in?"

For a moment Adolphus did not answer, then he said, "She be sleeping. She do much business today. You go leave her, there be other girls."

"I want her," Painter said. He moved towards Adolphus threateningly as if he intended to strike him.

Adolphus looked at him distastefully, then he shrugged his shoulders and led him to a door at the end of the corridor. Painter took the lamp he was holding, opened the door and went inside.

The room was small and grimy, and a dirty, faded curtain was hanging across the middle of it dividing it into two smaller cubicles. There were two narrow beds, and on one of them the little girl from the Rivers lay curled, sleeping as quietly and peacefully as a child. When the light from the lamp fell across her face she opened her eyes and sat up. She said something in a frightened tone in her own language, but when Painter put down the lamp and came into the light where she could see him, she smiled.

He took off his clothes quickly, and went and stood over her. She was wearing a wraparound, and when he caught it and pulled it off her, he did it so roughly that she almost fell off the bed. He took her just as roughly, letting himself fall on top of her so that their bodies smacked together, and causing the girl to rear up off the bed with a cry of pain. He thrust himself deep inside her, and began to ride her hard, grinding her down, and the savagery of his blows made her turn and twist her head on the pillow and moan in fear. The sounds of their breathing and the sucking whack of their bodies filled the little room, and in the lamplight their shadows moved monstrously about the walls.

When he felt himself beginning to come, Painter tried to draw away, but the girl held onto him, and he discharged explosively inside her; and it was as if everything had been drained out of him, all anger and frustration and pain, and he was like an empty shell with no more need or longing.

After a time the girl pushed him awkwardly aside and sat up. She looked at the blood on the sheet, then she got

109

off the bed and cleaned herself. When she came back she stood looking down at Painter. He was lying on his back with his eyes closed. She went over to the lamp and turned it down, and then she sat beside Painter on the bed. She stayed like that, smiling quietly into the darkness, until the first light of dawn pushed feebly at the windows. Then she too lay down and slept.

Part Two

GETHSEMANE

1

In March 1968 Onitsha was captured, and in April the Federals took Ogundizzy. On a morning made cold by the Harmattan wind, they came silently and quickly, appearing out of the dawn mist which enveloped the lake, and by the time that the sun had nudged its bloodshot way above the horizon they were advancing through the town.

They met with no opposition, for the Biafran soldiers had already scuttled their only gunboat and had melted away like ghosts into the bush and mangrove swamps to the south. There was nothing they could do; they were outgunned and outnumbered, and to stay and fight would have been foolish. They were not brave men, but neither were they cowards; they merely wished to survive. They were farmers and ex-students, shopkeepers and small businessmen – only the officers were regular soldiers – and they knew that the Federals too would run away if they were not bolstered up by all the magic of British Saladin armoured cars, Russian mortars, and full bellies. The war in Biafra was like that, it was full of noise and fury and high-flown proclamations of defeats and victories, but at the centre it was hollow. It was a small, mean war, and the appearance and sound of the guns caused more destruction than the actual shells that they fired. Fear and rumour were the apocalyptic horsemen which moved the thousands of refugees from one place to another and caused them to die in agony from the twin cancers of despair and starvation. In the beginning the dream of nationhood had hovered bright and steadfast, and perhaps the leaders still believed in it, but now after almost a year of the reality of war the people saw the dream for what it had become: a nightmare of confusion, a landscape of surrealism and distortion, where nature had gone mad and children became gnarled obscene caricatures, where men and women appeared like walking skeletons, where suppurating wounds and charred emaciated bodies were ordinary sights, and where people wept, not out of the depth of their anger, but rather out of uselessness and self-pity. There was no more virtue, greed and avarice were paramount, and the rotting carcass of a bony pi-dog, or a handful of groundnuts, was something to be fought over or to be sold at an exorbitant price.

The people of Ogundizzy had not so far felt the full brunt of the war, but they had been inundated by hordes of relatives who had, and this had caused them to become lethargic and secretive, and mistrustful of their neighbours. When the Nigerian soldiers rounded them up and made them watch while they took Igor, nailed him to his own front door, and set fire to him, they stood passively and made no protest. If the act was meant to cow them, then it was unnecessary, for they were already full of fear. For many months they had been frightened of the unknown, and any reality, no matter how bad, can never be as terrible as that which the imagination is able to conjure up. In truth, it had the opposite effect of making them feel easier in their minds, for they were relieved that someone else should suffer for them. They had never been particularly fond of Igor, he had worked himself and them too hard, but now they were grateful to him, and perhaps one or two of them may even have felt some sympathy for his agony.

By ten o'clock the town was completely quiet. The soldiers occupied the more solid and impressive looking houses, and their owners were driven out and forced to go elsewhere. The door of the priest's house was broken in, but the house was deserted and the small altar had been dismantled. The soldiers found a crate of beer under the stairs, and some wine; and they drank this and threw the bottles against the walls. They found the Mass vestments and tore them up, and two of them fought over a small chalice that they found locked away in a drawer. Later in the morning a number of the girls of the town were raped and someone set fire to the Welfare Hotel, but otherwise the Nigerian soldiers caused no more trouble than the Biafrans had.

In the middle of the morning the officer in charge, Captain Innocent O. Basanji, commandeered Igor's large American car and drove up the hill to the school.

2

Painter lay on the bed and looked at the ceiling of his bedroom. He did not turn his head when he heard the noise of the motor car engine, and when it stopped outside his house, he shifted on his side and turned his face to the wall. He lay inside the mosquito net, fully dressed except for his shoes, and his white shirt was sweat stained under the arms and down the middle of the back. He had been lying there now since early morning, since his boy, Jude, had awakened him with the news that the Federals had arrived. He knew that it would only be a matter of time before they came for him.

There was a knock at the door, and then a louder banging when no one came to open it. Someone shouted, a sharp authoritative sound, and then there was the crash of breaking glass, and Painter shuddered as he heard the door being forced open. He turned and looked through the mosquito net at the man who walked into the bedroom.

He was a small neat man in a carefully pressed uniform. His hat was set squarely on his head and he carried a short stick like a riding crop in his right hand. His boot-heels came together with a sharp click when he stopped just inside the doorway. He looked at Painter for a moment, then he jerked his head and said, "Get up." He did not wait to see if his command had been obeyed, but went back outside.

Painter got out from under the mosquito net and looked at his face in the mirror beside the bed. He looked pale and rumpled, and the pillow had left a red mark down his right cheek like a scar. He brushed his hair ineffectually with his hands and then sighed and went out into the living room. The other man was standing by the door, he was holding one of Painter's books in his hands and seemed completely absorbed in it. After a moment he said, "I read a lot. I do not find it relaxing. Rather it keeps my mind active." He glanced at Painter, then he closed the book with a snap and threw it on the table. "Novels, however, are not my favourite form of reading. I think I enjoy biography more than any other type of writing. At one time I thought of becoming a journalist. It would have enabled me to meet so many great men."

"I believe they sometimes have feet of clay," Painter said. He leaned uneasily against the table and saw with surprise that he forgotten to put on his shoes.

"So I am told. I would find that most disappointing, especially if I had wasted my time in admiring one such. I do not like to waste my time on nonentities."

Painter picked up a packet of cigarettes from the table, took one out and lit it. He saw that the other man was watching him, so he offered him one. With another of his abrupt movements the Captain raised his stick and knocked the cigarettes out of Painter's hand. Painter was so startled that the cigarette in his mouth also fell and hit the ground in a shower of sparks.

"I am Captain Innocent. O. Basanji," the other man said, and he smiled at Painter's discomfort. "You are?"

"Michael Painter."

"Well, Mr Painter, I want you to know that your being here is of no help to me whatever. As a matter of fact, it is a positive embarrassment."

"Why?"

The Captain smiled again. His face was round and soft and did not quite match his small muscular body. He had

117

a good smile, it even reached to his eyes. "Would you like to sit down?" he said, ignoring Painter's question. "You look tired. Do you not sleep well?" He might have been a doctor inquiring after his patient's health.

"It's difficult to sleep in this heat."

"But surely at night it is quite cool? Now that the Harmattan is blowing ..."

"It was late before I got to bed."

"You were reading?" The Captain bent down and gathered up the spilled cigarettes. He put them back in the packet and placed it carefully on the table. "Or perhaps you were writing?" he said. "It is difficult sometimes to remember unless one writes something down."

"I was neither reading nor writing," Painter said. He lowered himself into a chair and stared at the ground. "If you must know, I was drinking."

The Captain removed his cap and placed it also carefully on the table. "Do you drink to forget?" he said. "Or do you find that it gives you courage?"

Painter shrugged. He looked up at the Captain, but the sunlight in the doorway slanted across his face and blinded him, and he had to move sideways in order to bring him back into focus. He thought of how he had told Father Manton two days before that he had finally made up his mind to leave Nigeria, but like any decision that does not require action at the time of making, it had continued to plague him. He had tried whiskey as a cure, and the night before he had drunk a full bottle; but when dawn had broken in its usual silent splendour he had still been sitting, cold and desolate, with the remains of his depression still littering his mind like shards of broken glass. He said, "If you had come tomorrow, I would not have been here," and it sounded like a reproach.

"I would have preferred it if you had been gone," Captain Basanji said. "There is no way now of sending you

118

away. We came down by river from Onitsha, and that is the only way open to us. We are encircled on all sides by Biafran territory; my men and I had to volunteer for this mission."

"Why did you volunteer?"

"I am an ambitious man. If I can hold this place for even a month I shall be a hero."

"Do you want that very much?"

"Of course, my career means everything to me. I was hoping for this war."

"There is much suffering."

"When one suffers then one is alive. I am never more aware of myself, my body and my mind, than when I am in danger. I had presumed that you believed this. Otherwise, why are you here?"

"I am here because of my inability to decide. I'm a victim of my own prevarication; I refused to tell myself the truth."

"Is that not true of everyone?" Captain Basanji said quickly, as if he too were afraid to hear Painter speak the truth.

"There are different kinds of truth. To lie to oneself must be the most foolish sin of all."

"Yet the most common?"

"Perhaps."

The Captain laughed. He walked carefully along the line of sunlight, his highly-polished boots clacking on the cement floor, then he turned and walked the three paces back to his original position. There was an economy of movement about him, a certain defined output of energy, as if any unnecessary action would be abhorrent to him, or would constitute a small fault in his make-up.

"What do you think of me?" he suddenly asked Painter, without changing the tone of his voice.

"You seem very well educated ..."

"For an African? Or perhaps you mean, for a captain in the Nigerian Army?"

"Your English is very good."

"You are an adept at avoiding questions. Perhaps after all it will prove interesting to have you here. At least, for a time."

"Why do you think I will be an embarrassment to you?"

"World opinion seems to matter in modern wars. This one is particularly well publicised. I may have to do things here which might not sound ... well, might not sound entirely correct, if you know what I mean. You may even be here for just that purpose."

"I assure you, I am not."

"Whose side are you on? Do you not sympathise with the Biafrans?"

Painter hesitated, then he said carefully, "I am on the side of whoever wins. I am no martyr, I only wish to go away. Far away," he added, as if he was afraid that the Captain would misunderstand him.

"You could have gone away long before now."

"Perhaps I thought that the Biafrans would win."

"They will fail."

"How can you be so sure?"

"They have only dreams, and a certain inbred cunning to sustain them. How can they resist an avalanche?"

"It's been done before."

"Not to my knowledge, and that is sufficient for me. I cannot fight with thoughts of failure uppermost in my mind. I am on the right side because I personally am strong and will not fail. My confidence is in myself, not in causes or pious aspirations, or in the vain mouthings of politicians. God is on my side because I am my own god. I need no other."

"And if you should be killed?"

"Killed! I shall not be killed." Suddenly the Captain had lost his temper – "Take care," he shouted at Painter. "You are closer to death than I am. If an accident were to befall you then I would no longer have to worry about what you see or do. I hold your life in my hand. I am your god also."

Painter stared open-mouthed at him, his face pale and grimy with sweat and his eyes sick and full of fear. He put up his hands as if to shield himself from the other's anger, and when the Captain raised his stick he felt a loosening in his bowels and he almost cried out.

The Captain stood over him for a moment, then he lowered his arm and slowly smiled. He took one of the cigarettes from the table and lit it. He blew smoke meditatively into the sunlit room, then he put the cigarettes and matches into his pocket and started to pace up and down. To Painter's surprise he said, "I want you to like me. As you say, I am well educated. Educated people should at least respect each other. At the moment I can see that you are afraid of me. But with time that will change. When you get to know me better you will appreciate my virtues. It will only require a little effort, on both our parts."

"How long do you intend to keep me here?" Painter said. He sat back in the chair and put his hands on the arms. He could feel the sweat run down his body, and he thought longingly of a shave and a shower. His attempt at a beard had not lasted long. It had seemed to him too much like a badge of involvement, as if he had taken out shares in a venture which he knew from the start was doomed to end in catastrophe. The Biafrans grew their beards in imitation of their leader, he had no such reason for growing his; a beard is one of the oldest forms of disguise, and almost always the one most easily seen through.

"Who knows?" the Captain answered his question. "I presume you will stay as long as I stay. If the army attacking Onitsha manages to break through along the road, then we will be here for the duration of the war. If not, then I will have to retreat as soon as my supplies run out. If you wish, you can try to get as far as Uli, but it would be a hazardous journey, and you would have to do it on foot. The Biafrans might take you for a mercenary and shoot you."

"There are no mercenaries. Don't you know that? It has been officially denied by both sides. This is a private war, not like the Congo."

"There is no such thing as a private war. War is common property, it attracts all kinds, like flies to honey. It provides an unlimited opportunity for killing, for gain; it enables the strong to assert themselves and those who were born to be victims to sacrifice themselves. It is one of the greatest ways of allowing the human spirit to wallow in extremes."

"You speak like a philosopher rather than a soldier."

"I read that somewhere," Captain Basanji said, dismissing his remarks as negligently as he swung the baton that he carried. "Wars should not be philosophised over, they should be fought and fought well."

"That's all very well providing that only the experts: the soldiers and planners, suffer. Unfortunately millions of innocent people also die."

"They do not matter, they were born to die in such a way. They would not have amounted to anything. There will always be others to replace them."

"You haven't much regard for the nobility of life."

"There is very little nobility in the sight of ordinary human beings grubbing out their ordinary little lives. My mother was a bush woman who could neither read nor write. My father had three wives and could support none of them. I was taken to Lagos as a child by my uncle, and he left me to fend for myself when I was ten years old. I lived on Victoria Beach and slept in the sand, and my sole possession was a broken umbrella which some rich whiteman had probably thrown away. I fought and stole and sold myself to survive, and there was nothing noble about anything that I did."

"Do you not think that there was something admirable about the fact that you did survive?"

"No. I was taken by the Fathers and sent to school and then to the Military Academy, but I survived because I was meant to survive."

"But the Fathers' gesture in caring for you was surely proof of their nobility?"

"Why? They didn't do it for me, they did it for themselves. They were satisfied that they had saved another soul for God. I was merely another feather in their caps, another step on their way towards Heaven."

"At least it was Christian."

"How can you say such a thing?" The Captain looked agitated, and he began to pace up and down again. "I am not a Christian. They did not convert me to anything. I was one of their failures. Can't you see? I despised them. They were ugly little men who smelled bad, and if I pretended to pray and to believe in their teaching it was only because I needed them at the time. None of what they taught me gave me any peace of mind – The peace that surpasseth wisdom – I laughed in their faces when I graduated as an officer. One of them, he was Irish like you, he told me that he was so proud of me, of how I had pulled myself up from being nothing and now I was an officer in the Nigerian Army, with a fine starched uniform to wear and a future stretching ahead of me. He was congratulating himself, not me. I went out that day and bought the most expensive umbrella I could find, and I gave it to him. I had paid my debt, I owe neither him nor his God anything further." The Captain came and stood in front of Painter and looked into his eyes.

"You remind me of them," he said. "I had to confess to them just like I'm confessing to you. You are soiled like them, and you are white, and you have the same worldly indifference about you. The people told me that you were not the priest, but I begin to doubt them. Have you got

123

your book of prayers hidden away somewhere? Are you sure you're not a man of God?" He spoke the last words with a look almost of hatred on his face.

"Like yourself, I'm not even a Christian," Painter said. "I profess to being a Catholic, but now I only pray when I'm afraid and when I sometimes sense the emptiness of my unbelief. I envy you your certainty."

The Captain raised his hand and struck Painter in the face. He did it without warning, a full deliberate swing of his arm, and the slap of it in the silence of the room frightened Painter as much as the pain. He fell back in his chair and put his hand in front of his face, but the Captain did not strike him again. Painter took down his hand. Another red discoloration bloomed on his cheek to join the one already left by the pillow. He began to feel very sorry for himself.

Captain Basanji straightened up and moved away from him. "That was only a small lesson," he said. He seemed pleased, as if he had forced something out of Painter against his will. "You must remember the situation that you are in," he went on. "If I do not trouble you, and allow you to move about freely, the people will think that you are collaborating with the enemy. It is for your own good that you remain here, at least on the school compound."

Painter said nothing, and the Captain smiled at him. "Do not sulk," he said. "I could just as easily have you shot."

"No." Painter shook his head. "You wouldn't do that."

"Why?"

"Because you are just as afraid of me, or at least what I represent, as I am of you. You cannot afford to have me killed."

"And what do your represent?"

"I'm white. It's not as easy to explain away the body of a dead whiteman as it is of a black. It would be a bad mark

124

against you, and I think you care about that. You'll make certain that I stay alive."

"Then why are you afraid?"

"I'm afraid because you may destroy me more surely than if you had me shot. I might even grow to like you, as you said."

"How could I destroy you?"

"By making me believe what you believe, by filling me with hatred so that I would lose what little humanity I may possess."

"You over-estimate yourself. Are you so much better than I?"

"Yes, because I can only succeed in fooling myself now and again. No one can live on hate alone."

The Captain looked puzzled. He said, "I do not know you. I have never met you before. How can you presume to judge me? We have conversed for only a short time, and yet you profess to know me enough to form an opinion about me. I'm disappointed in you. Could you not have given me a little more time before you arrived at your conclusions?"

Painter looked at him, then he turned his head away. "Yes," he said softly, "perhaps I'm blaming you for my own faults. I'm sorry, I can only put forward the excuse that I am tired."

"Thank you," Captain Basanji said, as if he had won a minor victory. "Perhaps you will think differently when we meet again."

He picked up his cap from the table and settled it carefully on his head. He walked to the door and then turned and looked back. "Would you like to come and eat with me tonight?" he said.

"Yes," Painter replied, but he showed no great enthusiasm, and the Captain went on. "It might be better if I came here. Is your boy still about?"

"I imagine he is. Where would he have gone?"

"He might have gone for bush. Most of the young men have disappeared."

"There are stories of atrocities."

"Fear is a great deterrent. We have to safeguard ourselves somehow. And the atrocities have not all been on one side."

"Is that how you justify them?"

The Captain went to the door. He said irritably, "I do not need to justify anything to you. I have talked to you at length this morning only because I felt like it. It is merely a matter of luck that you caught me in such a mood." He looked at Painter over his shoulder. "I shall be here at nine," he said. "I would advise you to stay inside your house today, my soldiers are not as well disposed towards talking as I am. Perhaps you could spend your time in prayer," he added, and he smiled again vaguely before he went out into the sunlight.

3

Captain Basanji waved away the driver of the car and, instead of taking the road towards the town, he walked down in the direction of the school compound. The sun was high in the sky and it was very hot, yet the Captain did not sweat. He was as neat and fresh as when he had first set out that morning. He took great pride in his appearance; it was as much a badge of his office as his uniform, or the stick that he carried. He knew that his men admired and respected him; perhaps they even feared him a little, but he also knew that his hold over them was as tenuous as a cobweb, and as easily broken. Some of them were regular soldiers, but the great majority were young men who, before the war, had aimlessly walked the streets of Lagos, scratching out a meagre existence as best they could. Anyone could hire them for a small sum to do almost anything, and their respect for human life and property was non-existent. In former days they had worked for the politicians. They were called thugs, and even the police were afraid of them. Since Nigeria had gained her independence in 1960, a number of elections had been held, each one more crooked than the one that went before it, and the thugs had played a very important part in those elections. The whole way of life in Nigeria at that time was based on a complicated system of bribery, or dash as it was called, and any wealthy man could become a politician if he felt like it. One of the first things that he did, when thoughts of higher office came into his head, was to hire his own personal army of toughs. They persuaded the people how to vote, and they clashed with rival gangs when the occasion warranted it. When the army had taken over, one of their stated aims was to abolish this system of dash, but the thugs had become very powerful and difficult to put down. The outbreak of the war had solved the problem, for the thugs had been inducted into the army, and now they could carry out their former way of life even more freely than before.

The Captain came to the bottom of the hill, went past the deserted dormitories and climbed the rise towards the main school building. His booted feet kicked up little swirls of red dust with each step he took, and when he looked up, everything before him seemed to change and to shift in the shimmering waves of heat: the dusty palm trees, the monolithic anthills, the large rambling building, the whole scene, seemed to swim and dance as if gripped in the throes of a silent earthquake. He felt as if he were walking into a rippling painted canvas which billowed away from him, and a slight feeling of nausea made him quicken his pace, until he came gratefully into the shade of the stunted trees guarding the front of the school. He had started the morning in very good spirits, but now he felt slightly annoyed with himself, without knowing exactly why. He had enjoyed talking to Painter, yet he knew that he had given too much of himself away. There had been something so familiar about Painter, with his grimy aura of tired perplexity; he had radiated a sense of desperation which had made the Captain over-confident of his own position, and yet, by the end of their conversation, the Captain's mood had undergone a subtle change, which he could not comprehend. Was it that Painter had communicated some of his uncertainty to him? he wondered. Had he, in some inexplicable way, managed to shift part of his troubles onto his, the Captain's shoulders? It was always the same with whitemen, he thought: one never knew the extent of their

128

strength or weakness, and by the time that one found out, it was usually too late.

He began to walk along the length of the stone corridor, and the sound of his footsteps rang out slow and solemn in the stillness. The doors and windows of the classrooms were closed and shuttered, and dust had blown in, and was hard and gritty underfoot. He stopped opposite one of the doors and he kicked the wooden plank that had been nailed across it. It was dry and warped from the Harmattan wind, and when he kicked it again, it splintered, and part of it came away. In a sudden frenzy he began to kick at it with both feet, first the left, then the right, driving his heels into the dry wood until it came away completely, and the door sagged backwards on its hinges. He shoved it fully open and went inside.

The room was still dark, only one shaft of sunlight came in through the broken door and it illuminated the teacher's desk like a spotlight. He began to tear the shutters from the windows, ignoring the clouds of dust, and relishing the noise, and the feel of the splintering wood in his hands. He did not stop until he had opened all the windows, and when he had finished, he felt a feeling of elation, as if he had done something really worthwhile. It had been so long since he had engaged in anything so purely physical, in anything which had given him so much satisfaction at the cost of so little. He looked about him, at the rows of empty desks, at the silent, badly painted walls, and the sunlight seemed to invade his mind, just as it filled the quiet classroom, and he allowed the sensation of release to sweep over him like a stream of brightly flowing colour.

After a moment he went and sat in one of the desks. It was too small for him, but he wedged himself in and looked at the blackboard. An idea came to him, and he got up and walked to the top of the room. He found a piece of chalk in a broken cupboard and, slowly and carefully, he wrote his name:

129

Captain Innocent O. Basanji,
on the blackboard. He stood and regarded it gravely, then he stepped forward and wrote under it:

Colonel Innocent O. Basanji.

General Innocent O. Basanji.

President Innocent O. Basanji.

He put his head on one side and said the words aloud, savouring them as if they were the names of exotic foods. He hunted about and found a duster and rubbed them out. Then he wrote in their place:

Father Innocent O. Basanji.

Bishop Innocent O. Basanji.

Pope Innocent O. Basanji.

He turned on his heel and faced the empty classroom. The dusty sunlight gave the place a solemn, faded appearance, and the motes of chalk-dust floated in the air like pollen. Slowly he raised his hand and made the sign of the cross, and it was as if something which had been hidden away inside him for a long time had broken free and was hovering in the dimness near the ceiling like a black cloud. He began to laugh, softly at first, and then more harshly, and the sound echoed through the deserted building and broke against the walls in waves of discord.

4

It was seven o'clock before Jude returned, and when Painter told him that the Captain was coming to eat there that evening he looked frightened and said there was no food. Painter leaned against the doorway of his bedroom and watched the boy move about in the lamplight. With the coming of the Biafrans the electric generator had ceased to function, and soon the oil, too, would run out. The Federals had made an attempt to repair the generator, but just before they had arrived Igor, perhaps in a fit of patriotic fury, had put sand into the mechanism. Now even Igor's house, like the remainder of the dwellings in the town, hid itself away in the silent anonymity of the night; it was now a poor place to visit. Painter had often wondered if Igor was crouched inside, with his host of wives and children about him, as frightened as the other men of the town, for whom he had once had such contempt.

Jude finished making the bed and started to pull the net down over it. He took the flimsy material carefully in his fingers, working slowly and tucking it in around the corners, as methodical as a young wife putting away her bridal veil. He had been with Painter for five years, coming first as a very small boy with a shaven head and bearing a note from the Sisters to say that he had spent some time with them training to be a cook. He had been shy almost to the point of speechlessness, but he had finally managed to convey, in his very bad English, that his name was Jude and that he was twelve years old. Against the advice of

131

O'Rourke, Painter had taken him on, and at first he had regretted it, for the boy was completely unable to cope. He was a poor cook – one of the first desserts he had put before Painter was a tin of tennis balls which he had roasted in the oven – and he was also lazy. But Painter had persevered with him, for after he had got over his initial shyness he had proved to have had a winning smile, and when his hair grew, he turned out to be quite handsome. They had gone through many vicissitudes together; at one stage the boy had begun to steal, small things at first like cigarettes and beer, and later, money. On a number of occasions Painter had threatened to fire him, but he had always relented and taken him back again. He had never really asked himself why he kept the boy; he knew that he could get much better cooks for the same amount of money, older men with wives and children and responsibilities, men who would carry out their duties quietly and well. One evening, a couple of months after hiring him, Painter had asked him if he liked working for a whiteman. "It is no matter," the boy had replied, making Painter wonder if he had mistreated him in some way, but later he had realised that Jude had merely said what he thought would satisfy him. No whiteman had probably ever asked the boy that question before, and if he had, he had certainly not bothered to listen to the boy's reply. Why should he, Painter, be any different? Later, when the boy made mistakes or stole from him, Painter had remembered his reply and had been ashamed to tell him to leave.

Now he straightened up from his work and looked at Painter across the lamplit room. He was wearing only a pair of old blue shorts and there was a slick of sweat along his shoulders and across his chest. "I am afraid," he said apologetically. "This afternoon I hide for bush. I only come out when night falls. These foreigners be very bad men. This morning they chopped Igor proper."

"You mean they killed him?"

"Yes. First they burned him, and then they cut off his head. It be sad too much."

"Sweet Jesus," Painter said, and he thought of Captain Basanji's highly-polished boots and his bright ingenuous smile. Had he stood and watched, and smiled his smile, while his soldiers tortured Igor? Is that what he meant when he had said that atrocities were necessary because they engendered fear? Painter looked at the boy in front of him, then he said, "Was Igor the only one, or were there others?"

Jude shrugged and did not bother to answer the question. Instead he said, "I no stay here now. Tomorrow I go for bush again, and this time I no come back."

"Stay for one more night and prepare this meal for the Captain," Painter said. "After that it doesn't matter. I would have advised you to go anyway. I hope that I shall soon leave myself."

Jude nodded, but he lingered on and said, "I not want to be part of these troubles. Why must I go and hide for bush when I be in my own place not have done any bad thing? Why do these soldiers come to drive us away?"

"I have no answers to your question, Jude," Painter said. "Why must anyone suffer? The Church teaches that it is because of the sin of Adam and Eve that the human race lost paradise. We share in a universal guilt which must be expiated. Surely you learned that in your catechism?" he added, but he knew that his answer was useless. What good were abstractions to Jude, or to the millions like him who were being forced to suffer by a dream of freedom so intangible as to have made no difference to them in the past and which, even if achieved, would have no effect on them in the future either? What did freedom mean to people like that? Was it the right to live in peace and prosperity, and to die of old age, surrounded by relatives and friends? But that was the most impossible dream of all. Peace and prosperity

133

were words which had no meaning at any time or in any place; only one word had meaning, and that was exploitation: even the weak exploited the less weak by their demands for protection and support. What gave the boy the right to expect him to be able to explain away his fear? Why should he be put in the position of having to justify something which he personally was not responsible for? Painter felt the anger well up inside himself, and he began to feel ashamed, for he knew that his anger should have been directed against the forces that had led the boy and himself into that predicament, and not at Jude himself. He said gently, "I'm sorry. I wish I could tell you why these things happen, I wish I could say that everything will be all right. At least you are alive and you have food to eat." He stopped and gestured hopelessly, and the boy, believing perhaps that he was being offered consolation, came and stood against Painter's body.

For a moment, in the quietness of the room, they stayed like that: barely touching, while the cloth of the mosquito net shivered in the night air, and the darkness pressed almost palpably against the windows. Painter's body sagged forward, and he put his hands on the boy's shoulders as if he would gather him close against him; it was an involuntary movement similar to the boy's, a stirring of some old longing which now reasserted itself like the siren of a distant train, carrying him back to childhood, carrying him back to a time when his mind was free of shadows, and the needs and responsibilities of growing up were gathered together and dissolved in the smell of woodsmoke and the boyish healthy length of summer days. He felt a delicious quickening in his blood, and a slow motion sense of well-being as if time had no more dominion; he saw all of his past life, all the seconds and the minutes, the hours and the days, being brought together and blended into a single pulse-beat of contentment the like of which he had never before experienced. He felt the heat of the boy's body and smelled his musky odour, and with this perception of the sentient cause of his momentary obsession, like the slow falling of a star came the realisation that he was no longer young, that he was in fact behaving like an ageing pederast, and that the guileless unrealism of his youth was lost to him forever.

He pushed Jude away from him and looked forlornly about the room. Once more he could hear the monotonous chanting of the crickets, could feel the humid breath of the tropical night, could taste air which felt as if it had been breathed by too many people too often; and he listened to the singing in his head die away like a whisper of regret. He looked at the face of the boy – was it a disappointed face? Had his need betrayed him also to the point where a moment's fumbling on a bed with another man would have given him some form of release? Would it have left any stain on his innocence if they had attempted some type of sexual coupling, some physical act which might have sublimated their anxieties in a wave of grunting groaning effort? Painter put out his hand again, this time with the genuine intention of comforting the boy, but Jude merely gazed at him uncomprehendingly. The moment was gone, lost in time, and perhaps it had never really existed; the need for something is sometimes sufficient in itself, fulfilment can often bring its own dissatisfactions, and desperation is sometimes preferable to indifference. Painter felt his anger return, but this time it was anger at the shabbiness and triviality of his own imagination. His grubby surroundings, the grime, the sweat, the sordid stale atmosphere, they all epitomised for him the mediocrity of his thoughts and aspirations; his mind was small and enclosed, its boundaries were diffused and blurred in a greyness of tired clichés and spurious dissimulation. Was there ever a time, he wondered, when it had been different? A time when he had really been true to himself and to the world about him? He remembered reading somewhere that a man should aim at the stars, and if he then managed to get to the top of a high mountain, he could be satisfied with his endeavour; he could only see himself shouting into the wilderness from the tops of little hills. He thought: how does one lose one's way for the first time? Is it by getting up and walking away when the world whispers in one's ear? There should be something to signify that the time had come for a pact to be made – a blinding flash of light or a chorus of celestial music – it wasn't fair that man should be left to grope about in such a fog of uncertainty and unease. And if the pact was broken there should be no more need for thought, or memories, or even fear.

Painter let his hand fall to his side and he forced himself to smile at the boy. Why frighten him further by acting out of character? He was used to a master who only spoke to him about things that he could understand: the toughness of the Hausa beef, the absence of water for a shower, the small discrepancies in the household money at the end of each month – ordinary everyday things which kept familiarity at a distance and of themselves meant nothing. It was better thus.

"We must get some food somewhere," Painter said. "I wouldn't like to displease the Captain."

Jude shrugged his shoulders. "It not be possible," he said sulkily. "Only some small amount of beans and yam remain."

"You'll have to do the best you can."

Painter took some money out of his pocket and offered it to the boy. He knew it was not enough, but it was all he had. Of late he had not worried very much about money, there was very little that one could buy with it other than food. Now he realised that without it he was in danger of starving, just like the thousands of others. The knowledge

136

that he had finally become part of the brotherhood of suffering brought him little consolation, it was merely like the crisis of a sickness, something that had to be endured until health returned or, he realised with a shock, until death intervened to take away the pain.

The boy went out and Painter wandered aimlessly into the other room. He took up a book, the same novel that Captain Basanji had held in his hands earlier in the day, but he soon put it down again and resumed his pacing. Tonight his mind was strangely active, it was as if it had become rejuvenated by a long period of passivity. He felt elated – was it possible that he was looking forward to the company of the Captain? To the company of a man with a mutilated mind? Or was it simply that he needed someone to talk to, someone who would fill an empty space with his presence and not merely be an echo chamber for his own half-formulated scraps of thought? He felt the place on his cheek where the Captain had struck him. Could it be that he might achieve revenge? Might humiliate the Captain by showing him that good must ultimately take precedence over evil? Usually he shield away from argument, but tonight he felt that he would welcome it. He thought of O'Rourke, and of Father Manton who had gone away on retreat just two days before the Federals had arrived, and finally of Ben Nzekwe, and for the first time he felt no equivocation about his decision to stay in Biafra. He was sure now that he had a part to play, and the knowledge, like a small but steadfast flower, took root in the stony soil of his will and bolstered up his flagging sense of hope.

He went out onto the verandah and along the gravel path which bisected his overgrown garden. The stars trailed a filmy haze of brilliance through the sky, their usual hard glitter overlaid by rags of cloud, and the night was as still and deserted as a sports arena after all the crowds and athletes have gone. From the hilltop the town was a deeper

137

blackness against the surrounding countryside, and no lights showed. He moved slowly along the pathway, his feet kicking up little spurts of silver sand in the starshine, and the soft susurration of his movement was no more than a whisper in the darkness. He walked across the road and along by the empty wards of the hospital. The nuns had left soon after Christmas, journeying unwillingly into Owerri in the back of a Mammy Wagon, and their patients had faded into the bush, some of them being supported on bicycles and others carried on the backs of their relatives like tired children. They would now have to rely on the ministrations of native doctors, providing of course that the doctors themselves were not too full of sickness and disease to care for them. The nuns had been victims of their own vows of obedience: they had not wanted to go, but the Bishop had decided that his responsibilities towards them could best be effected if they were close about him in Owerri. He had also, at the time, made one last attempt to entice Painter into leaving. He had sent him a letter, in tone that of an angry parent, to tell him that this was perhaps his last chance of leaving. Father Manton had been almost apologetic when delivering it; he at least had seen that any further argument was useless.

Painter came out on the gravel path in front of Anne Siena's shuttered house and stood for a moment looking back over his shoulder at the way he had come. He went over to the front of the house and sat down on the cracked steps leading to the door. The undergrowth had crept back around the house like a thief stealthily approaching his unsuspecting prey, and the carefully-tended garden was now no more than a miniature jungle. He thought of the girl with regret, and remembered how he had allowed her to leave without going across to say goodbye. He had been unable to face her after the last night together, remorse and shame had combined in equal measure to keep him away, and when he had heard that she was gone he had felt a secret relief, for he knew that if they had met he would have again experienced the same old half-felt sentimental fantasy of idealistic love which had ruined their relationship before. He believed now, as he had also believed then, that he was the one who had been mainly at fault; from the moment that he had become aware of her as being more than merely an acquaintance he had built her into something that she most certainly was not: namely, an integral part of that social fabric which his background had always led him to believe meant security – a steady job, his own car and house, money in the bank, but above all, a neat respectable wife. It was something which had always trailed him down the corridors of his mind since he had come to the age when it was deemed right and proper that he should settle down. After all, was he not a normal Catholic Irish boy and did he not need the fulfilment of a wife and children to stabilise his position in the Catholic ethos? He had always fought against this idea, he found its smug acceptance by so many of his age group an abomination; yet, with some other, some softer part of his mind, he had craved it. To be conventional, to fit in, to fill all the lonely days and nights with multitudes of trivialities, that was what he sometimes longed for with an equal mixture of desire and hate. His coming to Africa had been his way of opting out, but he could not opt out of what he was, and he had carried his love-hate with him like a cancer which he was unable to kill or cure. Suddenly the phrase, 'a fate worse than death', came into his mind, and he grinned and shifted his position on the hard cement step. Yesterday he would not have been able to laugh at his dilemma; perhaps it was a sign that a cure was setting in in spite of all.

He stood up and stretched his arms above his head and, as he did so, he heard a sound from the side of the house. It was a tiny irritation, a scratching or scraping like crisp paper being opened, but it sounded very loud in the silence of the night. He slowly put his arms down and looked about him. For the first time he noticed that the ground near the corner of the house where the sound had come from appeared to be moving; it seemed to pulse and sway before his eyes, and the small rustling noises now became clearly defined for what they were. A nest of soldier ants was on the move, myriads of the small scuttling insects weaving a carpet of animated excitement as they went towards the corner of the house; and they were disturbed about something, for instead of travelling in their usual ordered columns, they had spread out, as they do when they are agitated.

Painter moved hurriedly away, skirting the gleaming, clicking incrustations as best as he could, yet a small number of the insects managed to crawl up under his trousers and sink their stings into his flesh. He brushed them off and stood to one side to watch the tireless activity. Once, some years before, he had awoken one morning to find that a nest of them had invaded his bedroom; they completely covered his mosquito net, hanging in clusters like some form of sickly artificial fruit, and when he had run in terror from them they had fallen about him like miniature bombs. Yet they had a strange, insidious fascination for him, like the crawling things that are sometimes uncovered when a rock is overturned, and, instead of walking away, he moved around the house in an effort to see where they were going.

The house was a long low bungalow. Its walls, which had once been painted white, were now stained and mottled by years of rain and sun, but they still gleamed palely in the starshine. Someone had attempted to plant yams in a small plot of ground, but this was now overgrown by weeds, and the yams themselves had gone wild and had broken through the ground like monstrous, misshapen heads. Painter put his feet down gingerly, thoughts of snakes being very much on his mind, and he kept close to the side of the house until

140

he got to the far corner. He hesitated for a moment, as if fearful of what he might see, then he slowly leaned forward and looked at the scene in front of him.

Sitting crookedly against the drab wall of the house was the body of the deformed old nightwatch who had so carefully looked after Anne Siena when she had lived on the compound. The ants must have just discovered him, and they were methodically devouring what remained of his devastated body. They crawled all over him, two lines of them streaming from the empty eye sockets like discoloured tears, while others of them carried away bits and pieces like robbers rushing from a grave.

Painter was appalled. He stared at the scene, his mind registering the grisliness of it, but refusing to accept it. He felt numbed, as if he had been given a massive anaesthetic to guard him against some future pain. He had asked for a sign, a warning – was this to be it? This travesty of a human being which now moved slightly under the pull of the ants, but which retained its fixed grimace of a grin even as it was being slowly eaten.

Suddenly a great weight of feeling broke inside him; it welled up out of his throat as an agonised, moaning keen, and he turned and ran blindly away from the horror in his mind's eye. Panic-stricken, he fell among the half-buried roots in the ruined garden, but he continued on, scrambling on his hands and knees through the undergrowth, until he emerged once more onto the gravel pathway. He hauled himself shakily to his feet, the breath rasping in his throat and the nausea in his stomach making him dizzy, but the vision of corruption that he had just seen still loomed large before him. He began to run again, his legs pumping beneath him, faster and faster, and when he could go no further he fell on his face in the dusty road and lay like a man who, having crawled across a desert towards a shining city, gets there to find nothing.

After a long time he arose and brushed the dust from his clothes and went back across the road. At the top of the hill the lighted windows of his house bloomed in the darkness, and he moved towards them slowly. A small gathering of fireflies winked above his head as he walked.

5

Captain Basanji arrived promptly at nine o'clock. His driver followed him in carrying a bottle of Vat 69 whiskey with a faded label, and a large pineapple which he took out to the kitchen.

The Captain looked at Painter, who was sitting in a chair directly under the light, at the sweat on his face and his crumpled slept-in appearance. There was a smudge of earth on the shoulder of his white shirt, and he looked like someone who had returned from a long journey and had not had time to wash and to change his clothes. The Captain wrinkled his nose – "You have been out walking?" he inquired. "I told you to remain in your house today."

Painter shrugged and said nothing. The mood for talking had left him and he could think of nothing to say. The Captain continued gazing at him, then he too shrugged and began to open the bottle of whiskey. The binding around the neck of the bottle was loose and came away easily, and when he took the cork out with a soft plop, the room was filled with the bitter smell of Kai-kai, the native gin. Painter looked at him in surprise and then began to smile at the expression on his face – it appeared that someone had still enough courage left to sell him a doctored bottle of whiskey. "Did you buy it from someone in the village?" Painter said almost gleefully.

The Captain stared at him, then he slammed the bottle down so hard that some of the liquid shot out and spattered on the floor beside his feet. He called out, and his driver came in from the kitchen. He was a large ungainly man, with a flabby, stupid face and a slack grin. He had forgotten to button the flies of his trousers, perhaps he had been urinating and the angry tone of the Captain's voice had caused him to come in too quickly. Now he stood and looked foolishly from one to the other of them.

The Captain said something to him in his own language, and his mouth dropped open even further. He looked around him as if he expected to see someone else in the room, but when he saw no one he gazed at Painter with a strange expression on his face. He waddled across the room and went outside, and when he came in again he was carrying a large revolver which he handed to the Captain. He went out reluctantly, still staring at Painter over his shoulder.

Captain Basanji put the gun on the table, where the lamplight winked along its blue-black surface and softened its sharp contours so that it looked like a child's toy. Painter stared at it, but it awoke no emotion in him. The Captain's gesture had been too banal – it reminded him of an old movie, where the villain seeks to bully a crowd of extras gathered round a table, but one knows that the hero will soon enter and outdraw them all. The Captain must have sensed something of this, for he said mildly, "I like to have a gun near me, it has so many uses." He might have been talking about a tinopener or a pocket knife.

"We can still drink it," Painter said suddenly, indicating the bottle of Kai-kai. Strangely, the Captain's discomfort had broken his own mood, but he did not wish to argue anymore; now he wanted a quiet, peaceful evening and to talk about only trivial things, so he said, "I'm afraid that the meal may not be the best. It's almost impossible to buy food of any quality. I tried to get some eggs," he finished lamely, "but there were none to be bought."

Instead of answering him the Captain took a neatly

144

pressed handkerchief out of his pocket and began to wipe the neck of the bottle. When he had finished he poured out two drinks, and he picked up one of the glasses and moved away from the table, but he did not sit down. He walked about for a moment or two, then he went and stood with his back to the door, as if to show his contempt for the darkness and what it might contain.

Soon Jude came in with the food, and they sat and ate in silence. The meal was tolerable – soup, curried chicken, roast banana pie – the boy had worked a minor miracle in being able to procure so much. Painter was glad that he did not have to offer any apologies, for he wished to retain some trace of self-respect in the face of the Captain's ill-concealed sense of superiority.

They drank the Kai-kai with the meal; it tasted a little like kerosene, but after the first few mouthfuls it lost a lot of its sting and became almost palatable. When they were eating the pie the Captain called Jude in and told him to bring them the pineapple. "And put your shirt on," he told the boy, as if he, and not Painter, was master of the house.

Painter had half expected that the fruit, like the whiskey, would be rotten inside, but it was quite delicious; perhaps whoever had sold it to the Captain had been trying to make up for the spoiled liquor.

When they had finished eating they remained on at the table drinking the remainder of the Kai-kai. Jude had lit some candles in order to conserve the kerosene in the Aladdin lamp, and the small flames, steady and unwavering in the dry air, looked pale and forlorn against the brightness of the starlit sky outside the windows. It had grown cold, and Painter shivered with a chill which the raw alcohol did nothing to alleviate. He said, "Even Kai-kai loses its taste after a time," – but the remark sounded forced, and exactly what it was meant to be: merely an effort to break the silence between them. The Captain shifted in his chair; he creaked as if he were encased in cardboard, and the idea gave Painter an almost uncontrollable urge to giggle. He said quickly, "I heard that Igor was killed this morning?" – but the manner in which he framed the question left him with a vague sense of shame. The horror of Igor's death deserved a more accusatory inquiry than the question he had asked.

The Captain did not answer. Instead he said, "On my way here tonight I saw a girl. She is waiting for me now back in my quarters." He paused and stared at Painter. "You would like a woman tonight?" he asked him.

"That too can lose its taste," Painter said. "Tonight it would simply be a form of masturbation. I feel no desire, no need except perhaps for the sexual act itself. Surely there should be something more."

"Are you talking of love?" The Captain leaned forward and spoke into Painter's face: "I have heard so much of this love. I have read about it, and I have seen it portrayed in films. Does such a thing really exist? According to the Fathers who taught me, it is comparable to the emotion we should feel for God. I have never felt it, either for God or for woman. When I mount a woman I feel hated, a fine wild hatred which sings in my blood like the beating of drums. There is no tenderness, no desire to kiss or to talk. Why is this so?"

"It's sometimes very difficult to distinguish between love and hatred," Painter said. "At least hatred is positive. It is preferable to boredom or indifference."

"Do not answer me like that," Captain Basanji said. He reached out and caught Painter by the front of his shirt. "Again you give me a priest's or a theologian's reply. We are men, answer me like a man. Do not pretend that you don't care."

"How can I tell you something that I do not know myself?"

"But you must know. You are a product of that culture

146

which has been imposed upon us Africans. You have succeeded so well that now we must try to live like you, yet inside we are hollow shells. We are the victims of something that has not come from within ourselves; we are the victims of what you have given us so that we may be formed into your image and likeness. We speak your language, obey your laws, observe your religions; yet we are not allowed to think your thoughts or dream your dreams. Are we to be forever like small children, who must stay as they are and never grow up? You have led us into your type of civilisation, you have taught us how to wage war. Can you not also teach us how to love?"

"Perhaps that is something that you must learn for yourselves."

The Captain released him, and Painter leaned back in his chair. "You ask too much of me," he said. "I've become so accustomed to thinking in clichés that now I can find no other way of answering you. Have you never said to yourself after being with a woman. 'This is good, this is something that I have to have again'?"

"Of course, but it is the act, not the woman, which stirs this emotion in me. The woman is merely the instrument of my passion. I have had many women, they are all the same."

"But has it not at times been better with some women than with others?"

"Yes, but again it depends on myself and the amount of hatred that I feel."

"Hatred! How do you know that it's hatred that you feel?"

"How do I know! I know because I live with hatred. I feel it in the middle of battle, I sleep with it at night and I awake full of it in the mornings. I have always known it. It has brought me through many dark hours when I felt that the sun would never again shine. I depend upon it like a lame man depends upon his stick, and it has enabled me to be strong and to survive. Can love do that?"

"Why are you telling me these things?" Painter suddenly cried. "Why are you asking me such questions?"

Captain Basanji stood up and placed his hands on the table. He bent forward until his face was close to Painter's. "Because I want you to persuade me that I'm wrong," he said. "One doesn't have to search for evil and corruption, it is all about. It is easy to see the weakness and the wickedness in people. It is not difficult to hate." All at once the tension seemed to drain out of him and he said in a gentle voice, "Have you never loved?"

Painter looked away from him and gazed at the stars blinking in the sky outside his window. After a long time he shook his head and turned back to the Captain. "No," he said, "I've never loved. I've gone through the motions, I've spoken words that I did not mean in the hope that I would eventually come to believe them, but it has never worked. I sometimes wonder if I'm incapable of love. Are you satisfied?" he asked the other man, as if he expected him to offer some form of comfort.

"No, I'm not satisfied," the Captain said. "You irritate me. You are the kind of man who preys on other people's strength and gives nothing in return. You are weak, and I despise weakness."

He picked up the gun from the table and pointed it in Painter. Holding it in his left hand, he reached out and extinguished the tiny candle flames, so that the only light in the room was given by the stars. His eyes shone in the dimness and, still staring at Painter, he called out something loudly in a hoarse, excited voice. His driver appeared almost immediately from outside holding a frightened Jude by the arm. The Captain spoke again, and the driver reluctantly released the boy and went over to the Aladdin lamp and lit it. The sudden flare of light surprised them all except the

148

Captain, who pointed the gun again at Painter, and stared at him without blinking.

Suddenly, without changing his expression, Painter started to laugh. It was an odd sound, like the giggle of an old man who has remembered some meaningless event in his past life and knows that he has no one to share it with except himself. The sound frightened the boy even more and he moved a pace or two towards the door, but the driver, progressing surprisingly quickly for a man of his bulk, waddled across and put his hand on his shoulder.

"You have a strange sense of humour," Captain Basanji said. He lifted the gun higher until it was pointing at Painter's left temple. "Shall we say that the condemned man laughed before his execution?"

The sound coming from Painter stopped abruptly, and he opened his mouth as if he were about to speak. He raised his arm but, before he had completed whatever gesture he had intended to make, his whole face collapsed and he began to weep. Tears ran down his face and dropped onto his shirt front, and he made no effort to brush them away. There were so many tears that they might have been stored up in him for a long time.

The Captain leaned down to him and whispered, "Don't you want me to kill you? Would it not be a logical cure for your lack of love?"

"No." Painter shook his head, and tears flew out from his face like spray. "I don't want to die."

"But why?" the Captain said. "Do you believe in an afterlife? Are you afraid that you will go to Hell?" He paused in simulated confusion, then he said, "Yet you told me that, as well as love, you lacked belief."

"I don't want to finish like this," Painter sobbed. "You've no right to torment me."

"I have the right. Strength gives me that right. I could destroy you as easily as walking on a fly." Once again he

149

paused. "But perhaps I don't hate you enough," he went on. "Killing you would give me very little pleasure. It would have no meaning."

The Captain straightened up and looked at his driver and the boy. He motioned with the gun, and the driver dragged the struggling Jude over to the table.

"Make your choice now," the Captain said to Painter's bowed head. He pointed the gun at the terrified boy, but Painter did not look up. "Did you hear what I said? The choice is between your life and the boy's. One of you has to die."

Painter raised his tear-streaked face. "This is not real," he said. "How can you threaten so dispassionately to take away a human life?"

"I am not being dispassionate," the Captain said. Almost desperately he went on, "You must believe me. I cannot retreat now from what I've said and done. You have forced me to this. Tell me that you hate me."

Painter shook his head. He opened his mouth to speak, but the Captain put out his right hand as if to stop him, and then he pulled the trigger of the gun. The explosion drove Jude backwards against the wall, and flecks of blood and flesh like coloured rain flickered through the lamplight. Painter's white shirtfront, his face, the Captain's hand holding the gun, the walls, the very ceiling, they were all spattered by the crimson spray. The boy made an indescribable sound and fell on the floor under the table, where he writhed about for a moment and then lay still. Painter, too, fell from his chair and came around the table on his hands and knees. He was making blindly for the door when he came in contact with the Captain's legs and, as if his strength had given out, he stopped and knelt against the khaki trousers like a penitent.

The Captain leaned down to him, still holding the smoking gun in his hand, and, in a shocked voice, he said,

"Don't you see? You made me do it. Let his death be on your conscience. I merely pulled the trigger."

"Jesus Christ," Painter said. He fell away from the other man's legs and grovelled about on the ground, trying frantically to wipe his hands and face in the matting, and when he opened his eyes, he could see the Captain's leather boots and, beyond them, the thing under the table that had been Jude. As he watched, a large red stain began to creep along the floor towards him, and the boy's left foot twitched once and then was still.

6

"But it's been almost three weeks," Father Manton said plaintively. "Someone will have to go and find out what is happening. Why shouldn't it be me?" He sipped some water and gazed at the food on his plate, but his appetite, which had never been great, seemed of late to have deserted him completely. He picked listlessly at his portion of chicken and said again, "Three weeks, anything could have happened in that time."

"Anything, or nothing." His superior, Father Ossermann, stared across the table at him. "As a rule they don't kill whitemen. Besides, if you go you may be captured. Then there would be two of you to worry about." There was the tiredness of repetition in his voice, as if he had had to go over the same argument again and again, and now found that it was beginning to bore him.

They were sitting in the refectory of the seminary at Owochukwu, a long, low room containing three rough wooden tables and a number of benches worn smooth by the succession of students who had sat on them over the years. The main building dated back to Bishop Shanahan's time, but the refectory had been built on later as a kind of afterthought. On the green painted walls hung pictures of Popes who had long since died: sad, careworn faces, the faces of men who must have found very little humour in their lives; perhaps sanctity and laughter are incompatible, like true justice and mercy.

Father Ossermann looked enviously at a neighbouring

table, where the pilot and the co-pilot of the latest relief plane to fly into Uli Airport were sitting. They were eating and drinking noisily, their drawling Australian voices giving the room an unaccustomed air of vivacity so different from the constrained aura of silence which usually enveloped the seminarians who ate there. He would have liked to have gone and sat with them, to have partaken, however vicariously, in the barely-suppressed sense of heightened awareness which always seems to be generated by men who are doing something insecure and hazardous. He lit a cigarette, absentmindedly forgetting to offer Father Manton one, and said through the smoke, which hung motionless in the air, "The Biafrans will soon recapture Ogundizzy. It's only a matter of time, and then we will know one way or the other. If anything has happened to Painter," he went on rather sharply, "it's entirely his own fault. He was advised often enough to leave."

"I know, I know," Father Manton said, "but we cannot throw off our responsibility just like that. And it's not merely Painter that I worry about; the people may be suffering."

"But what could you do if you did manage to get through?"

Father Manton shrugged his thin shoulders. He said awkwardly, "I have a duty to be there. They were my parishioners. Why should Painter stay on, and not me?"

"Circumstances dictated his remaining there. It was pure chance. You told me yourself that he had decided to leave the country. If the Federals had captured Ogundizzy just a day later then he would have been gone."

"But that makes no difference to the fact that he is there and I'm not. I should be with my people."

"They are not your people," Father Ossermann said irritably, but he immediately regretted his remark, and he said, "I'm sorry. What I meant was that all the Catholics in Biafra are your people, not just those in Ogundizzy."

153

"Surely not just the Catholics?" Father Manton gazed suspiciously at him, as if he feared that Father Ossermann's sense of charity was not as all-embracing as it might have been.

"Yes, of course, all the people. But could we not, just for the moment, confine ourselves to those in Ogundizzy?"

Again he regretted his sharpness, and he began to wonder once more why the Bishop had chosen him, at this troubled time, to be his representative among the Fathers in the area. He knew that he was not a gregarious man, and he had never pined, like some of the other priests, for the closer ties and the active sublimation of parish work. Neither had he tried, like Father Manton, to be both pastor and educator. His work teaching mathematics in Na'wadi High School had left him with a lot of free time and he had used this to lead an ascetic life, and it had suited him very well. Perhaps the Bishop had seen in him a good administrator and had thought that his aloofness would be mistaken for strength; but the Bishop had always been a bad judge of character, his views and feelings being of a simplistic nature, and the fact that Father Ossermann was disliked by the other Fathers probably led the Bishop to believe that he was content to be disliked. Fastidiousness and austerity, however, can quite often be merely a shield to hide a painful shyness, or the inability to communicate with others, and he was honest enough with himself to know that his eremitism was sometimes a penance which he found hard to bear. It was not difficult for him to understand Father Manton's wish to be back among his parishioners, but he knew that if it were he himself, he would be inwardly relieved not to be a part of a situation about which he could do nothing. But now he had run out of arguments and, as he again gazed at his companion across the table, all he could think of, and all he could once more say, was, "What help could you be to the people? Or to Painter?"

"Perhaps my being there would be of some help," Father Manton answered. "Perhaps the fact of my voluntary arrival among them might cause a raising of their spirits." He looked a little ashamed as he spoke, as if he felt that Father Ossermann might think that he was making himself out to be a hero. "I wouldn't be harmed," he went on hastily. "There would be no danger."

Behind them the door opened, and Father Sanson, who was in charge of the unloading and the distribution of the relief supplies, came in and walked across the floor to them. He paused beside their table and said, "I hope I'm not interrupting, but we'll soon have to go. It's almost time for the midnight plane."

Father Ossermann looked at him gratefully and said in a relieved voice, "I'll drive you down myself." He gazed at the two priests in front of him: at Father Sanson, so young and so full of life, his enthusiasm for the work that he was doing making his manner towards the two older men almost hostile by its insouciance and its implication that they might possibly be wasting his time – he was plagued by no intimations of inadequacy or self-doubt; and at Father Manton, his face thin and lined, and every facet of his appearance plainly displaying his uncertainty in the face of the burden which he was being asked to carry. Am I seeing the birth and death of idealism? Father Ossermann wondered. Is optimism merely an adjunct of youth, and does it leave only its shade behind to torment old men? Perhaps the greatest fear as one grows older, he thought, is that hope, too, will die before the heart stops beating. He stood up and forced himself to smile at Father Manton, and as he said, "Come along with us, it will take your mind off other things," he could feel the paucity of his words like a sour taste in his mouth.

As they drove towards the airfield the Thames van jolted and swayed on the rough dirt road, and the headlights dipped wildly across the trees and small clusters of houses that they passed. Father Sanson and the two Australians sat together in the back and talked and laughed among themselves, but Father Manton stayed hunched forward grimly in the front and said nothing. Father Ossermann was aware of his silent presence, but he made no attempt at conversation. He gave his full attention to the road, visualising in his mind the more dangerous bends and rougher patches before they actually appeared, and enjoying the exhilaration of driving just a little too fast. He knew the road well; he made this same journey three times a week, and he knew exactly the spot where he would have to switch off the headlamps and continue on by the glow of the side lights alone. There were four checkpoints on the road, two of them manned by civilian militia, and the two nearest the airport by regular soldiers, but they had all grown used to him by now, and he was merely waved on at each one. As he passed the final one he flashed his lights once, and then drove slowly along the last few hundred yards.

The landing strip was merely a section of tarred road, widened and reinforced with concrete to enable it to stand up to the wear and tear of the heavy cargo planes. During the day it was camouflaged with bushes and fronds of bamboo, which had to be replaced each morning so that they would match the greenness of the surrounding area. There was only one building, a small corrugated-iron shed with no windows, and it was here that the business of the airport was carried on, with people coming and going and whispering into one another's faces in the smoky glow of one hissing Aladdin lamp. There was always a great deal of activity when a plane was due, but otherwise people were encouraged to keep away from the field, and most of the time it was deliberately kept deserted and unkempt like any other patch of jungle. Yet its location was well known, it was well publicised in the world press and it could easily be found on even the crudest map. There were conflicting opinion as to why it had not already been destroyed by Federal bombs: it was said that the anti-aircraft fire was too accurate to allow the Nigerian planes to come close, but probably the real reason for its preservation was that the pilots, who were mercenaries, did not wish to see it destroyed. The collapse of Uli would mean the end of Biafran resistance, and for the pilots who flew the Federal planes, it was a comparatively safe war, and a lucrative one. Therefore they contented themselves with buzzing the clandestine planes as they came in low over the tree tops, late at night; and the fact that some of the planes carried guns and other armaments made very little difference. The old-fashioned mortars and prehistoric small arms which were sold to the Biafrans by unscrupulous dealers from various parts of the world threatened little danger to men who travelled at heights of up to twenty thousand feet above the ground.

As Father Ossermann nosed the van in among the dilapidated Mammy Wagons that were standing about in the darkness, he wondered again at the fragility and utter dependence on chance of this lifeline of the Biafrans. Their ingenuity and happy-go-lucky attitudes never ceased to amaze him. They were fighting a war in which they were heavily outnumbered, both in manpower and in weapons, a war which was spread over a vast amount of territory, and yet they managed to operate a system of government which worked, and a fabric of social life which varied little from that which had gone on before hostilities had commenced. It was no wonder that they were known as the Jews of Africa.

Father Sanson and the Australians got out of the van and disappeared into the communications hut, and as if their arrival was a signal, the ring of landing lights, like a frieze of candles held by pilgrims, was switched on, and then

157

quickly off again. This dot-dash system would be operated until the incoming plane had either safely landed or had decided that it was too dangerous to come in that night.

Father Ossermann got out of his seat and stood beside the truck, where he was joined by Father Manton. A soldier came across to them and ordered them to take off their white soutanes, and, feeling a little foolish, they did as he instructed. Hovering high in the dimness above them was the broken wing of one of the planes which had crashed. It, too, was camouflaged, so that it looked like a natural outcrop of rock, or perhaps a large tree which had become rotten and had tilted over sideways. Two Americans had perished in that particular holocaust, and the small wooden crosses which marked their graves now joined the other crosses which showed where those who had died before them lay.

Father Ossermann felt no thrill of anticipation as he heard the drone of the incoming plane reverberate faintly from the darkness of the sky. He had no further part to play, he was merely the driver who made certain that the people who were really important arrived safely. Now he waited around like an uninvited guest: he was the spectator at a funeral who turns his head this way and that in search of a familiar face, and only offers consolation from a distance. He looked around for Father Manton, and was surprised to find that he, too, had disappeared into the night. Has even he found something useful to do? he wondered. He made a sudden movement, walking blindly forward like someone who is afraid to be alone by himself in the darkness, but then his foot slipped on a root, and he realised how foolish he was being. He looked up as the roar of the approaching plane's engines became louder, and then he could see it above him, swooping shatteringly out of the night sky and settling down thankfully between the double rows of tiny flickering lights. At least that much had been accomplished safely: the plane had landed, and soon he would be able to drive a jubilant Father Sanson back to Owochukwu, and for someone the night would have been well spent.

7

Father Manton shifted his weight in order to favour his left leg, which had lately begun to trouble him. He was standing near the landing lights, out where the road narrowed once more, and as the radiance flashed on and off across the face of his companion, he tried to remember where he had seen him before. He was a young man, small and neat in his grey army uniform. There were badges of rank at each of his shoulders, but Father Manton had never been able to distinguish between the various insignia, and now he said, "How long more must we wait, Lieutenant?" deciding that "Lieutenant" was probably the most likely appellation; and either he was correct or the other did not bother to put him right, for he answered him immediately and said, "You must be patient, Father. They will come eventually."

Father Manton had been standing near one of the Mammy Wagons when the soldier had first tapped him on the shoulder and told him that he had an injured companion who was in need of a priest. He had followed him unhesitatingly for, with the scarcity of medical facilities, it was not unusual for a wounded soldier to remain with his companions until he either got well or died.

They had stumbled along in the darkness, past the groups of patient people silhouetted against the lighter shading of the sky, following the edge of the runway until they had come to where they were now waiting. The plane had landed and had been unloaded – from where he was Father Manton could still see the tiny figures running to and fro as they stacked the various bales and boxes by the side of the shed – and now the old Dakota was preparing to take off once more. He felt a vague stirring of unease; he had imagined that the wounded man was somewhere close by, in one of the mud houses of the natives perhaps, but now he realised that they were probably waiting for some means of conveyance to take them further afield.

The plane turned about and rumbled towards them and, just when it appeared that it would overrun the lights and crash into the forest, it rose into the air and swept away over their heads. The sound of its departure had scarcely died away when the noise of a vehicle of some sort came to their ears. Father Manton peered about him, but he was looking in the wrong direction when a Mammy Wagon came to a grinding halt beside them. It had come from the airfield, rather than from the north, and this surprised him, although he did not really know why it should not have come from where it did.

Before he had time to argue he was helped up into the cab of the truck, and it started off again up the road. The driver, a fat man wearing a coloured cloth around his head, was bent forward, leaning over the wheel and squinting at the road in front of him. He drove without using any lights whatever, and he must have known the way very well, for it had begun to rain and the night was as black as pitch.

They rattled along for some time, the heavy truck slamming down with a crash into every pot-hole they met, and once they had to stop while a barrier was removed from across the road. The rain began to come down more steadily, and it blew in on top of Father Manton through the windowless door of the truck. He had left his soutane behind him at the airfield, and the thin shirt and trousers he wore afforded him little protection against the chilly moist air. He knew the part of the country through which they were travelling quite well, but with the rain and the darkness he soon lost all sense of direction, and when the truck suddenly lurched to a halt, he presumed that they had merely paused to have some other obstacle removed from the road. He sat shivering in his seat while the driver got out and disappeared into the murk and gloom of the night.

For some time he was alone, only the patter of the rain on the roof of the truck and the wet rustle of the bush disturbing the stillness, yet he felt no sense of strangeness. On many nights like this, in the past, when he had been called out by the local catechist to visit someone who was sick and in need of the last sacraments, he had sat like this in the rain. Before he could enter the house he had to wait outside while the catechist went in to see that everything was in readiness. This was the ostensible reason given for the man's entering before him, but Father Manton knew that in reality he went in first to make certain that all traces of the Ju-ju were removed, so that the priest could work his spell undisturbed by rival gods. He had often felt, as he knelt over the wasted body of some dying person, that he was bargaining for the soul just like someone at a sale endeavours to snatch away some object from under the nose of a fellow shopper. Many a time upon leaving he had been tempted to look back, hoping to catch an anxious relative whipping away the white cloth, and the statue of the Virgin, in order to accommodate a new offering, perhaps a bunch of withered twigs, or a beer bottle full of some evil smelling liquid.

He had been crouched in the truck for what seemed an interminable time, when he heard the small sounds of people speaking quietly, and the young soldier who had first approached him suddenly appeared out of the rain and stood looking up at him. It was only then that he recognised him, and he realised that it was the man's new found air of authority which had prevented him from knowing who he was before this.

162

"You can come down, Father," he said. "We have reached our destination. It be only a little way further, but we must walk." His voice was polite and full of solicitude, but there was a firmness about his grip as he helped the priest down from the truck, and he held onto Father Manton's arm as he began to feel his way forward in the darkness.

They stumbled along slowly, their feet squelching in the mud of the road, and when Father Manton spoke, he felt compelled to whisper as if they were doing something secretive and slightly dangerous. "It's Nzendi, isn't it?" he said, sensing without seeing the other's nod of affirmation. "I didn't recognise you at the airfield. Of course I only caught a glimpse of you," he added. "Otherwise I'd have known you immediately." He remembered rather guiltily how he had first employed Nzendi to teach in the school at Ogundizzy. He had not been too eager to hire him, for he had an unsavoury reputation so far as women were concerned, and it was rumoured that he had badly injured a girl of twelve by forcing her to submit to him. But he was from the village of Ogundizzy, and Igor had seemed keen to have him taken on, so he had employed him. He had only been working there a matter of months when the school was taken over by the army, so it was impossible to know if he had been a success at his work. Now Father Manton tried to keep his former dislike out of his voice as he said, "Could you tell me where we are? I'm afraid I lost track of where we were travelling. Are we near Orlu?"

Nzendi mumbled something in reply, but the priest could not make out what he had said; and then he saw that it did not matter, for they were approaching a group of dark buildings, and by their size he knew that they were in a school or mission compound. A door opened in one of the buildings, a narrow rectangle of yellow light like a hole in the darkness, and they sidled through into a room whose dimensions were lost in the dimness outside the circle of

163

light cast by an Aladdin lamp. A number of men were sitting about, some of them barely visible in the shadows, and again it was impossible for Father Manton to know how many were there, or who they were. The lamp was on a desk whose surface was scored and furrowed, as if legions of people in the past had scratched their initials on it, with the hope, perhaps, of leaving something of themselves behind after they had gone; and as Father Manton stared at Colonel Ozartu, who was sitting across the desk from him, he felt obliged to say protestingly, "You should not have deceived me. I thought I was on a mission of mercy."

The Colonel said nothing, but drew deeply on a cigarette, which he held carefully between the two middle fingers of his right hand. As the smoke curled about his head he looked through half-closed eyes at the priest, and then motioned with his left hand at a large cushioned armchair which looked incongruous beside the plainness of the desk.

Father Manton sat down, and he immediately felt at a disadvantage as he sank into the cushions. He gazed back over his shoulder at Nzendi, who stood slightly behind him, and the smile that greeted him, and was probably meant to reassure him, only added to his sense of uneasiness. The others in the room, the grey shapes that he could barely discern in the dimness, all of them appeared to be watching him, and he felt as if he were on trial for something which he knew nothing about. The cushions in the chair creaked as he shifted position, and he was relieved when the Colonel suddenly smiled at him and said, "You are on a mission of mercy, Father. But we have to talk a little first." He stopped and slowly lit another cigarette, carefully holding the glowing end in the match flame until it was burning to his satisfaction. His movements were deliberate and rather ponderous, as if he had schooled himself not to rush too hastily at anything, as if the culmination of an action were to him something which must be delayed as long as possible in order to enhance the effect. As he lit the cigarette, he gave Father Manton the impression that anything that he did would have a certain rounded finality about it, an inevitability which would be devoid of complication or ambiguity, and which would require no explanations and no necessity for retraction. He would probably make a bad enemy, and perhaps an even worse friend; and Father Manton distrusted him even more now than when he had first met him in Ogundizzy.

Nzendi came forward and said something in Ibo, and when the flow of guttural words ceased, the Colonel smiled once more, but instead of speaking he leaned back in his chair and puffed again at his cigarette. Father Manton suddenly could keep silent no longer, and he said, "Why are you smiling like that at me? Why are you all smiling at me? I'm not a fool, tell me why you've brought me here." Something moved at the edge of his vision, and he twisted around in his seat, but everything appeared the same as it had been a moment before. He faced the Colonel again. "Are you trying to frighten me?" he asked him. "Why don't you speak? Why don't the others show themselves? If you want me to do something, then tell me what it is." He felt his face grow hot with shame as he added, "I'm a man of God, you have no right to keep me captive against my will."

Suddenly he stared as Nzendi put his hand on his shoulder, but he was not sure if the action was another attempt to reassure him, or an effort to keep him from jumping from his chair. "Be patient, Father," Nzendi said. "We must wait for a message. It should come very soon now." He patted the priest's shoulder, and Father Manton moved away from his touch as he would move away from some irritation, like a draught or a troublesome insect.

"There have been many changes since we last met, Father," Colonel Ozartu said in a conversational tone. "We have just heard that Port Harcourt has been captured. Perhaps you did not know?"

"No, I didn't know," Father Manton said, forcing himself to match the Colonel's calmness. "You are not surprised?"

The Colonel shrugged. "It had to happen. Our country is shrinking, but we will be able to defend a smaller area more easily. Perhaps all the towns will fall eventually. We will still have the bush."

"The bush offers little sustenance."

"But you yourself lived there for many years. You did not perish."

"I was one man, and I had no enemy to fight."

"No enemy, Father? Were you never tempted by evil spirits?"

"One fights the devil on the battleground of the mind. It's a question of inner strength."

"And you won?"

Father Manton felt that the Colonel was trying to trap him into making some admission which would leave him open to further attack. He said, "It's a struggle that lasts a lifetime. There are victories and defeats, and sometimes one is indistinguishable from another."

"Do you mean in your own personal battle, or in your fight for the souls of others?"

"It is all the one. If a man himself does not believe, how can he hope to convince others?"

"Then you have saved your own soul?"

"Only God can know that."

"So it is only after death that you can know if you have been successful or not?"

"I think so."

"It's a long time to wait."

"There are small compensations to be gained along the way."

"Such as?"

166

"The joy of seeing others being received into the true faith, and the knowledge that one has played a part, no matter how small, in their salvation."

Colonel Ozartu lit yet another cigarette. He said, "I am a Christian myself. It is good to belong to something which is so well organised. It gives one a feeling of security. Surely so many people cannot be wrong?"

Father Manton, who had been on the defensive from the start, suddenly looked outraged. He said heatedly, "How many people put Hitler into power? Men can always be wrong."

The Colonel looked at him with surprise. "Are you arguing against your own religion, Father?" he asked.

"No, against your reason for being a part of it. Do you not love God? Christianity was not created by man. It was given to him by God. The organisational side is only a temporal manifestation of the spiritual perfection that generated it." Father Manton was almost shouting, and the yellowish complexion of his features had become blotched and stained like used putty. His white shirt was beginning to dry, but in places it still clung to him so that the thin boniness of his torso could be seen, and the large brown spots on the backs of his hands were livid and ugly and might almost have been the remains of old sores. He looked like someone who had once taken some pride in his dignity, but now had fallen on hard times and did not care anymore. He said desperately, as if pleading with the Colonel to admit that he was wrong, "It would be so much easier if people trusted in God, if they believed and did not try to rationalise their belief. It is so simple: believe in God, obey Him and put yourself in his hands. Employees obey their employers, children their parents; every person invariably respects someone else. Why is it so difficult to love God?"

Colonel Ozartu turned away as if he could not bear to look at Father Manton any longer. He said, "You are speaking like a slave, Father. The human mind and heart will always question, will always refuse to believe that it cannot, of itself, attain perfection. God is mental and physical health, the joy of achievement, the song of success; and the devil is sickness and despair. I am a Christian through fear of being alone in a wilderness. I want beings like myself about me, for I think that the ultimate devil is loneliness." He held up his hand as the priest tried to break in. "I know there is nothing original about my thinking," he said, "but my reasons for being a believer are as good as the next man's. What does it matter if I see my neighbour singing the praises of God, and I refuse to join with him? How do I know what is in his heart, or he in mine? I enjoy the ceremonies of the Church, the pomp and circumstance, the multilayered order and harmony. Do not try to shake my faith by telling me to love God. I admire the elegance of His House, is that not enough?"

Father Manton had become quiet as the Colonel talked. Now he lifted his head and said, "I'm tired. I don't wish to argue anymore. Tell me what you want with me, or let me go. My place is not among soldiers. I am a man of peace."

"That's true," the Colonel said, "and I respect your philosophy. I merely want you to go somewhere with a few of my men. It will be a difficult journey, but you may find it worthwhile." He paused and looked sharply at the priest, then he said, "I'm sending you back to Ogundizzy. I hope you will not find that displeasing."

The priest returned his stare. He said, "No. As a matter of fact I would welcome it. But how can I go there? Surely the Federals are occupying the town?"

"They are. But that need not worry you. They will welcome you back as joyfully as the people. Many of them are Catholics, you know."

Father Manton looked disappointed. "Can it be as simple as that?" he said, but he was thinking aloud rather

168

than addressing the Colonel. He made a gesture of irritation, but then settled back in his chair. Perhaps the Colonel did have a magic wand that he would wave, he thought; perhaps the way really was open for him to return. No one would be able to say that he was not prepared to grasp at any straw. He was always ready to believe that the ways of God worked in a strange manner at times.

Colonel Ozartu leaned on the table. He said, "I am now only waiting for you to make up your mind, Father," but his tone of voice implied that he already knew that the priest would answer in the affirmative.

"I'm in your hands," Father Manton said, and yet the humble way he spoke could not keep a small note of excitement out of his voice.

8

The slow stain of dawn was already nudging the sky in the east when they came to the top of Ogundizzy Hill, but the rain and low hanging cloud would ensure that full light would be a long time in coming. "We must hurry," Nzendi said into Father Manton's ear, but his words were the words of someone who is talking merely to keep silence at bay, for the mud was almost up to the hubcaps of the lorry and the road in front got worse instead of better. "There is a roadblock at the bottom of the hill," he went on. "It is the only one." There was a note of contempt in his voice as he added, "These Nigerians are not soldiers, they are sheep. They know only how to sleep and to eat. When we kill them we will leave them to rot in the rain."

"This is a peaceful mission," Father Manton said sharply. "Don't talk of killing." He hugged the new white soutane that Colonel Ozartu had provided for him more closely about his body and tried to stifle the misgivings which arose in his mind like darts to assail him. He was sitting uncomfortably between Nzendi and the driver in the cab of the lorry, the same lorry that he had travelled from Uli in, and he felt sick and weary as if he had been travelling through a stormy sea in a small boat. Again he wondered if he had been wise to come on this journey – was it not a case of his having shelved his doubts in order to rely on the perfidy of man; but he consoled himself with the thought that, no matter what happened, no one could take from him the fact that he had tried. He thought, What more can one

170

do? ... and he allowed the question to envelop him, like a shield of reassurance.

The lorry lurched and slithered down the hill, the driver cursing in Ibo as he endeavoured to control it, and at one stage it hit the bank and almost tilted over. Soon the line of barrels across the road loomed up out of the dimness, and blurred figures could be seen, standing motionlessly in the gloom like patient hunters awaiting their prey. "Do you remember what to say?" Nzendi whispered anxiously, and Father Manton surprised himself by the steadiness of his voice when he replied and said, "I've only got to tell them the truth, it's lies that I find hard to remember."

They were still a good distance from the barrier when the driver applied the brakes, but the wheels could find no grip in the soft mud, and for a moment it appeared that they would crash into the barrels. The soldiers at the side of the road raised their rifles, and Father Manton felt the clutch of fear in his heart like the arrival of some old but mistrusted friend. The lorry slewed across the road and turned broadside on to the barrier, but it stopped before hitting it and the engine stalled with a sound like an exhausted sigh.

In the silence that followed, the soldiers outside prowled around the lorry suspiciously, none of them appearing willing to come too close. They held their guns pointing low, and the capes that they wore glistened slickly under the softly falling rain. They were like men who, having shot a wild animal, were still not convinced that it was really dead; and if the lorry had given the least shudder, or if the occupants of the cab had moved at all, they would probably have started shooting immediately.

One of them finally came to the windowless door and looked in at the three inside. Unlike the others, he carried a revolver, and he proved to be the officer in charge. He had a young face, and when he smiled, his teeth shone whitely in the murky dawn light. "Get down," he said. Then he added, "... slowly," and he pointed the revolver casually at the ground as if showing them the exact spot that he wanted them to step onto.

They got out carefully and stood with their backs against the lorry. The officer tilted his head and looked at them from under the peak of his cap. "It is not a good morning for travelling," he said. He smiled again. "We are grateful to you, of course, for breaking the monotony. We should really have shot you, but it is so lonely out here. Perhaps you would like to talk a little before we kill you?"

"I am a priest," Father Manton said, and again the steadiness of his voice surprised him. "My church is in the town. And my house." He indicated Nzendi. "This is my catechist. He and the driver volunteered to come with me. I wish to be with my parishioners. They have been too long without the sacraments."

"They will have to wait a little longer," the officer said. "They are patient people. I have not heard them complain."

"My business is not with you," Father Manton said. "I wish only to be allowed to go my way without hindrance."

"Who is your business with? God?" The officer turned and said something in his own language to his companions, and they laughed dutifully but without any great enthusiasm. He turned back and said, "My men do not appreciate your words. Would you like to work a miracle to convince them that you are a man of God?"

"Do not scoff," Father Manton said angrily. "You may one day have need of God's help."

The officer came close to Father Manton and, holding the revolver in both his hands, he put the barrel of it against the priest's neck. "Let Him come and help you now," he said. "Otherwise you will have no more need of anyone's help."

Father Manton stood up straighter and watched the finger on the trigger tighten. He thought: I can't end like

172

this; there is too much to be done and too much left unsaid. He looked into the eyes of the man in front of him, but they were merely angry and told him nothing. Beside him Nzendi made a small movement; and through the brightening air the rain swished down softly and glinted on the metal of the gun. To the priest the moment seemed like a spin-off from eternity; there was a crushing sense of time passing, and yet no time passed, and the amount of emotion that he experienced was like an apotheosis of all that he ever had felt, and possibly ever would feel. It was as if on the threshold of death he had suddenly come alive fully for the first time, and life, in all its infinity of possibilities, was at once more clear to him than it had ever been before. I can go on now, he thought; there is nothing further to fear; I am dying at the right time for the right reason, and my sacrifice is worthwhile because I know what I'm about to lose. He watched the finger on the trigger tighten even more, and then the hammer was coming forward and there was a hollow click like one single stroke from a metronome. The hammer had fallen on an empty chamber.

The officer laughed and took the gun away. "You were lucky, Father," he said. "God did come to your aid after all." He spun the cylinder of the gun, and four shells fell out onto the palm of his hand. "It holds six," he said. "The odds were against you. God must have a greater purpose for your life."

Slowly Father Manton relaxed, like a flower closing its petals, and against his back he could once more feel the rough wooden side of the lorry and the wet soutane clinging to his flesh. He dredged up a smile like a rictus of pain and said almost proudly, "You can't take anything from me. Even if you'd killed me you would have taken very little. It would have been a completely impersonal act. You would have been the one to lose."

"I'm afraid that I cannot look at it in that light, Father," the officer said. He looked about him, at the trees which were appearing from the dawn mist like sign posts of the new day, and at the rain which was still feathering its random way out of the grey sky, and he said with sudden urgency, "We've wasted enough time. When it's full light the Biafrans will start shelling us again. We must get back to the town."

Two of the soldiers had climbed up onto the back of the lorry, and they now threw out a long black box which settled into the mud with a soft plop when it hit the road. "What is this?" the officer asked, but Father Manton did not answer until Nzendi nudged him, then he said, "It's my Mass box. It contains my vestments and some altar wine."

The Officer made a signal, and one of his men forced off the lid and dumped the contents of the box out onto the ground. The gold facing gave the vestments a cheap, tawdry appearance as they spilled out into the mud, and the white linen of the alb thirstily soaked up the dirty-brown rainwater like a sponge. "Put them back," the officer ordered. He turned to Father Manton. "We will walk down into the town. Captain Basanji, our commanding officer, is now living in your house. He will not be happy to see you," he finished threateningly.

"Can we take the box?" Nzendi said, speaking for the first time.

"Why?" The officer looked at him suspiciously. "What is in it that is so valuable?"

Nzendi shrugged. He gazed at Father Manton, who said, "If your Captain allows me, I will say Mass. Then I will need the box."

"If you want it so much, then take it," the officer said.

Father Manton made a sign to the driver, but before he could move the officer said, "You are the one who needs it, Father; you carry it." He poked the driver with his gun, and then watched as two of his men lifted the box onto the shoulders of the priest. "Now we can go," he said.

They moved off down the road, leaving the lorry effectively blocking the hill, and in front of them the town grew out of the misty shroud of rain, and although it offered shelter it gave little sign of welcome.

9

"Igor is dead," Captain Basanji said impatiently. "He had an unfortunate accident. If he had not died perhaps there would have been many other deaths."

He looked with dislike at the bedraggled figure of the priest in front of him, then he sighed and walked to the window, but there was nothing to be seen except the rain and a section of deserted street. Behind him Father Manton said, "And what of Painter? Has an accident befallen him also?"

"Not yet," the Captain said, without turning around. He opened the louvered window and let the moist air play across his face. A fat woman came out of a house farther down the street, gazed for a moment at the sky, and then, straddle-legged, urinated like a horse onto the ground beneath her. The Captain grimaced and turned back to face the priest. He said, "Why have you really come here?"

"I've told you," Father Manton said. He looked around the room in which he had lived such a short time before. It was familiar to him, familiar in the way that a garment that one has once worn is familiar, but it held few memories. He said, "I wanted to be among my parishioners. They need spiritual care as well as every other kind."

"They would appreciate meat more."

"I can give them much more," the priest said defensively. "I can give them salvation."

"Just like that? What do you give them, a piece of paper with a divine crest on it, and your signature at the bottom?

176

... I guarantee that the soul of Joseph Okonkwo has been washed clean of all sin, that he has paid his alms faithfully on the first of each month, and that his children are all being brought up in the fear of God – signed Father What-ever-your-name-is. They should laugh in your face."

Father Manton shrugged painfully. His shoulders hurt from having carried the heavy box, and lack of sleep was beginning to dull his senses. He thought of his room in the seminary, of its stark simplicity and neatness; not so long ago it had overpowered him in a cocoon of claustrophobia, but now it seemed like a haven comparable to a palace. He wondered vaguely if the other priests had missed him yet.

"Well?" the Captain said. He brushed his short wiry hair aggressively with his hand and stared at the priest.

"Well what?" Father Manton said. He had lost track of the conversation. There was something else troubling him which seemed of greater importance, yet at that moment he could not think clearly what it was.

"Why are you here? Why did you come slinking in at dawn? Why do you arrive when the Biafrans are planning another attack?"

"I've already ..." Father Manton began, then the Captain's words sank in and he broke off. "How do you know that the Biafrans are about to attack?" he said.

"I know because it's my business to know. Are you trying to tell me that you have no knowledge of this? They have been using mortars now for almost a week. When the shelling stops they will attack."

"But that can't be true," Father Manton cried. He tried to think back to his conversation with Colonel Ozartus but there were so many other things going round in his mind that he found it impossible to concentrate. Surely the Colonel would not have sent him into Ogundizzy if he were meaning to attack it. What the Captain was telling him could not be true; he was merely trying to trick him. He

177

would have to be careful and say as little as possible. He thought helplessly: Please, God, let me not stumble now, not when I'm so close to being of some use once again. He straightened his shoulders and tried to look the Captain in the eye, but fatigue and old age had taken their toll, and he felt despair weighing on him like a great heavy shadow.

"It is certainly true," the Captain said. "It is merely a question of time. Perhaps it will be today, perhaps tomorrow. An attack is long overdue. I am surprised that they have allowed us to stay here for so long."

In spite of himself Father Manton said, "What am I to do?" and immediately he had said it he put up his hand as if to snatch the question back out of the air.

"Do! You may do as you please," Captain Basanji said. "I cannot care for you. You are not my responsibility. Go and join your fellow man of God on the hill. You can pray together for a better world."

"I don't know ..." Father Manton began dazedly, but the rest of his sentence was lost in the sudden clump of an explosion as a mortar shell burst somewhere in the town.

"You see?" Captain Basanji said. He moved away from the window and began to pace up and down. "You need not worry," he suddenly added, as if the priest had asked a question, "so far this house is out of range. But they are moving closer every day."

There were three more explosions and then a long silence, and for some reason Father Manton imagined the gunners standing about, laughing and talking, like men digging a hole in the road will sometimes stop in their work to comment on the people who pass by.

A soldier came in and began to speak in Yoruba to Captain Basanji. He seemed excited about something, and he said what he had to say quickly, and without pausing for breath. When he had finished the Captain gave him what

178

sounded like an order, and he went back outside, to reappear in a moment with Nzendi and the driver.

Captain Basanji turned to Father Manton. "So you came here to be re-united with your parishioners," he said. "What were you going to do, absolve them of their sins and then show them eternity? There's enough plastic explosive in your Mass box to send almost the whole town winging its way to heaven."

Father Manton looked at Nzendi, but he refused to meet his eyes. "I packed that box myself," the priest said. "There were no explosives in it."

"Well, there are now. The box has a false bottom." The Captain turned to the soldier. "Lock the priest up in the small room at the back of the house," he said in English, "and shoot the other two. Take them out into the open where the people can see you do it. They may have friends among them who have been awaiting their arrival."

The soldier began to push the two Africans with his rifle, but Nzendi resisted and said, "Wait." The Captain looked at him, and he went on, "I wish to make my confession. It will only take a short time. I have a grievous sin on my conscience, and it is troubling me too much. Let the priest release me from it."

The Captain smiled bleakly. "Do you really believe," he said, "that a man who carries explosives among his holy charms, and still proclaims himself to be a man of peace, has the power to forgive anything? What do you say, priest? Do you wish to work your magic over him?"

Father Manton raised his head, like someone who strives to raise a burden which is really too heavy for him to bear. He said dully, "There is always forgiveness."

"Even for you? This man has a reason for what he has done, he is a soldier of a type. You are merely a hypocrite."

"I was betrayed."

"Only because you were easy to betray. There is no one

179

as blind as a man with good intentions. Go and do your priestly work. I always imagined that it took a strong man to survive a solitary vocation such as yours. Your God must be very disappointed in you." The Captain looked at the driver. "Do you also wish to tell your sins?" he said, but the man stared at the ground and said nothing.

"He is a pagan," Nzendi said. "He knows nothing of the Christian God."

"Then let him die first." Captain Basanji turned his back on them as if they were beginning to bore him. "Lock the other two up for three minutes," he said over his shoulder. "Then take the catechist out also and shoot him. Leave the priest, it would not be a good thing for us to kill him. We will show him mercy."

He heard the shuffle of feet behind him, and when he turned around the room was empty. For a moment he almost regretted his last works to the priest: he had looked so old and vulnerable and, yes, so frightened. He thought of Painter, whom he had not seen now for a week, and comparing him to the priest he could find no great difference between them. They were both the complete antithesis of anything that he would ever wish to be. Suddenly he felt very secure in his own strength, both of mind and body; he had the power to destroy life with one flick of his fingers, and there was no one who could hold him to account. He stretched his arms wide above his head and yawned luxuriously. When the Biafrans attacked he would drive them away or kill them. There was nothing that was impossible, he felt, if one had confidence in oneself; and looking at it in that light, the world was made up entirely of conquerors and victims. He was a conqueror, and he would always be one, and if he did meet someone, or something, stronger than himself, then he would die gloriously rather than submit. That was the way it had to be, there was no other way.

A sudden commotion in the hallway made him turn his head. The young soldier who had taken the prisoners out, came in hurriedly and said, "Captain," and then paused as if he had forgotten what he had been about to say.

"Yes, what is it?"

The soldier looked frightened. He mumbled something, and then went back outside before the Captain could stop him. There was an outbreak of noise in the corridor, like people falling about, and then a silence that seemed to hum like a tightly strung wire in a wind. Captain Basanji got up and went out into the hallway, past the soldier who had called him, and past a number of others who stared numbly at him and then looked quickly away. A door at the end of the passage was standing open. He walked to the door and stood looking in. Father Manton and Nzendi were sitting on the floor opposite him, their backs against the wall, and they looked like two children who were resting for a moment from some game that they had been playing. Both of their throats were cut, and a small wooden-handled knife lay beside Nzendi's right leg. Blood was still flowing from the priest's neck and soaking into the front of his white soutane, so that he appeared to be gradually sprouting a ragged red beard. On the floor beside him his left hand clutched his breviary, and as the Captain watched, the fingers slowly uncurled and the book slipped quietly to the ground.

10

Later that day the Biafrans attacked Ogundizzy on three fronts. Just after dawn a number of them swam across the lake shielded by the high prows of water taxis. They remained in hiding until the main attack began, and then they infiltrated the town through the back door as it were. News of the priest's arrival had spread among the people, in that mysterious way that rumours have of seeming to seep out of the very air, and this information, even more than the impending attack, which they had known about for some time, stirred at least the surface of their waning interest. The women, especially, encouraged the men to take up their machetes, and to drift about in the wake of the soldiers giving them what help they could. Many of the men could barely stand up, for any food that had been in the town had been commandeered by the Federals, their own military rations having become exhausted in the first weeks of occupation. Nothing can take away a man's pride as quickly, or as surely, as seeing those whom he feels are dependent on him being abused in a completely impersonal and careless way; a blow struck in anger can be forgiven, but the coldly disinterested punishment is always resented. Now the men lurked in the darker byways of the town, their emaciated bodies giving them the appearance of patient vultures, and any wounded or disarmed Federal soldiers that they came across they chopped down bloodily like so many sheep.

The second Biafran point of attack was from the north, a direction from which the enemy would not expect them to come. All of this country as far as Onitsha was believed to be firmly in Federal hands; but they only controlled the main roads and the larger villages. The Biafrans were able to move through the bush as freely as they had ever been able to. They had even constructed a number of bridges over some of the smaller streams in order to transport their heavier equipment. Now they were able to come against the town from where it was least expected, and they fanned out and drove the few soldiers who opposed them back on top of those who were endeavouring to repulse the main attack.

The Federals did not have a chance. Some of them fought and died bravely, but many others, their morale weakened by the scarcity of food and the weeks of inactivity, simply threw down their guns and were butchered without making even a pretence of aggression. The officers grouped themselves around Captain Basanji and continued fighting, moving from building to building, until they were eventually hemmed in on all sides in the centre of the town. As the afternoon drew to a close, they too capitulated. Captain Basanji himself tried to fight on, but he was knocked unconscious by one of his fellow officers, and was captured lying on his face in the dust, ignominiously, and without having any chance of making the final defiant gesture that he had dreamed of.

When the body of the priest was found, the people demanded that the Captain should be given to them, and by the time that Colonel Ozartu arrived, the rain and the darkness taking away also his moment of triumph, the Captain had disappeared.

11

Painter chopped the small piece of yam carefully into wafer-thin slices, and he cursed viciously when he saw that the mould had eaten its way almost through to the centre. When he had finished cutting it up he began to separate the discoloured pieces from the rest, but then he shrugged his shoulders and dropped the whole lot into the small pot on the fire and poured some water in on top of it. The mould rose to the top and lay on the surface in a scum of blue dust, and the fire sizzled and almost went out as some of the water slopped over onto it.

He sat down on the floor and watched the food cooking. His face was smoke-grimed and had broken out in a multitude of small yellow boils, and his hair was long and matted and caked with dirt. Water was plentiful, for it never seemed to stop raining, but the general malaise of indifference which had overtaken him made the labour of washing and cleaning himself more irksome than the irritations that its absence engendered. He found a certain satisfaction in being, and feeling, utterly filthy; it seemed to him to be a passive protest against the set of circumstances that had brought him to it, and when the itching of his body drove him at times into a frenzy, he scratched himself almost joyfully until he bled.

He poked aimlessly at the food in the pot, and then sat back on his heels and let the knife fall to the ground. It had taken him a long time to find the piece of yam, for over the weeks and months since Christmas he had taken to hoarding any food that he could lay his hands on, often hiding it away so carefully that afterwards he could not remember where he had put it. The house smelled of stinking scraps – the day before he had found a rotten onion in his shoe – and at night the rats did not wait for him to go to sleep before they started scavenging.

He farted loudly, and then sat debating with himself whether a trip to the toilet would be worthwhile. Of late he had become obsessed with his bowels; if they did not move at least twice a day he became terrified, and would sit on the bucket in the bathroom for hours hoping for release. Otherwise time hung heavy on his hands, yet he never seemed to get anything done: two of the louvers in the bedroom window were broken and he had made no attempt to board them up – the rain blew in by day and by night, and the floor was continually awash: the candle in the water-filter needed to be changed: the mantle in the lamp was broken and shredded like a discarded lace curtain; he spent most of his waking time puffing and blowing at the smouldering fire in the kitchen, or lying on his soiled bed, or sitting on the toilet trying ineffectually to shit waste matter which was not inside him.

He found it strange, when he thought about it, that he felt no sense of loneliness. At first, in spite of himself, he had looked forward to Captain Basanji's visits, but after a time the man's company began to be a penance which he could well have done without. In an odd way he had begun to feel sorry for him, for the man's outlook, and his single-minded trust in his own efficacy, were as fragile and transparent – and in the long run, as boring – as the clever tricks of a precocious child. Perhaps one of the reasons for his half-premeditated descent into squalor and pediculosis was the fact that it helped to keep the Captain away. Now he was content in his solitary life – or perhaps content was not the correct word: he endured it, with a mixture of

185

resignation and righteous self-pity which took the boredom out of the ordinary small tasks that he had to perform in order to stay alive. Like someone travelling down into a dark and secret place, he had journeyed so far into a degradation of body and spirit that nothing could degrade him anymore; he could do the most trivial chores with an emptiness of mind and heart that bordered on the automatous, and instead of withdrawing into himself he seemed to be spreading out and becoming part of the prosaic environment in which he lived. There were times when, instead of eating some half-cooked morsel of food, he tipped it out onto the ground, and then sat staring at it, unable either to pick it up or to throw it away. At other times he gorged himself, stuffing the food so quickly into his stomach that he almost immediately regurgitated it, and could eat nothing for hours afterwards. He found himself getting into the habit of continually looking over his shoulder as if seeking for his shadow, and he became secretive, even with himself.

It was only at night, when he lay awake and listened to the rain sliding off the eaves of the house, or dozed fitfully in a welter of sweat, that the true horror of his situation manifested itself to him. Then he would pound his head against the pillow, and cry out in the depth of his fear, but no one ever came in answer to his entreaties. When he did manage to sleep he dreamed: great dark dreams of desolate wastes and gloomy shrouded landscapes, visions of echoing mirrored rooms with no one in them, and fantasies of whirling geometrical shapes which made no sound as they pulsed behind his eyes.

Now as he sat before the dwindling fire he began to hear strange sounds drifting into the room. At first he paid no attention, concentrating instead on the pot, from which all the water had boiled away and in which the yam had become a burned and blackened mass. It seemed very important to him that the sounds of the outside world should not impinge on the closed, tightly-knit routine of his existence, and he hunched himself even closer to the fire as the footsteps approached the door and the voice behind him said, "Mr Painter," in an interrogative tone.

He stayed as he was for as long as he could bear it, then he turned his head slightly and looked over his shoulder. Darkness had fallen without his being aware of it, but he could still discern the outline of the person standing in the doorway against the lighter blackness of the sky. He fumbled around on the ground until he found the stub of the candle, but the matches seemed to have vanished. Furiously he jammed the candle into the last few sparks of the fire, and then held it aloft when the wick burst into flame. The shadowy figure was wearing a soldier's uniform, and Painter said, "Captain Basanji?" but then he saw that it was not the Captain but a much older and heavier man. He was vaguely familiar, in the way that someone out of the distant past is familiar, and the sunburst epaulettes on the shoulders of his uniform showed that he was a Biafran, rather than a Federal, soldier.

"I have returned," the man said, as if at some stage in the past he had promised that he would, and he raised his eyebrows in an expression of inquiry.

"That's very good," Painter said dutifully, like a school-master commending a pupil for giving a correct answer. "Won't you sit down?" he went on awkwardly. "I haven't had many visitors lately." He waved the candle about helplessly: it was so long since he had engaged in polite conversation that he found it difficult to remember the right phrases.

"You don't recognise me?" the other man asked.

Painter hesitated, then he said apologetically, "Perhaps it's the poor light ... ?"

"I'm Colonel Ozartu. I was in command of the Biafran garrison here some months ago."

"Of course." Painter stood up and placed the candle on the kitchen table. "How are you?" He put out his hand, but then thought better of it and let it fall to his side. Suddenly he was painfully conscious of his appearance, and he began to feel a small pinking of anger towards the Colonel. The candle flickered and went out, and in the ensuing darkness Painter said grudgingly, "How did you get back? Did the Federals leave?"

"We have defeated them," the Colonel said curtly. "The fighting has been going on all day. Surely you heard the guns?"

"I heard something, but I've been alone for so long that it is not unusual for me to hear things. I put it down to my imagination."

"We have been waiting for many months for an opportunity to come and rescue you."

"Like the United States Cavalry?"

"Pardon?"

"I'm sorry." Painter made a gesture of apology in the darkness, forgetting that the Colonel could not see it. "Thank you very much," he said, but he could not keep a note of disbelief out of his voice which the Colonel was quick to note.

"A lot of planning has gone into this attack," he said, "and a lot of men have died in carrying it through successfully. Your friend Father Manton was one of the casualties," he added almost reproachfully, as if Painter alone were to blame.

"Father Manton?"

"Yes, Father Manton. Surely you have not forgotten him also?"

"Father Manton is dead?"

The Colonel sighed. He said, "The Federals killed him this morning before our attack began. They cut his throat and left him to bleed to death. He had come here to try to warn you."

188

Painter said nothing, and the Colonel went on, "Have you nothing to say? In a way he gave his life for you. He could have stayed away and not have put himself in danger."

After what seemed like an eternity Painter said, "He was an old man. It wouldn't have taken him long to die."

"Are you completely devoid of feeling?" the Colonel said, and he tried to peer through the darkness to see the other's expression.

"Feeling? I've been cured of feeling." Painter moved impatiently in the dimness. "Am I worth so much?" he said. "First the boy, now Father Manton. Could they not have died without involving me? Are they trying to hold me here, like a picture in a frame? Their deaths have no meaning. Why must I be the one to have to remember them?"

"Father Manton will be remembered by all of us," the Colonel said. "He was a brave man. He gave his life for his friends. He would have wanted to die like that," he added, and the note of sadness in his voice was so real that it sounded completely sincere; and perhaps he had really convinced himself that what he was saying was the truth, and that he was speaking the right epitaph after all.

12

The next morning Painter cleaned himself up a little and went down into the town. He felt like a recluse who had been dragged back unwillingly into the world by a set of circumstances beyond his control. Instead of experiencing a sense of freedom he felt hemmed in and unsure of himself; in many ways his period of isolation had been so safe, so secure – there were no responsibilities, no need to make decisions, except those of the most elementary kind, and there had been nothing demanded of him by anyone. Now he feared having to meet people again, feared having to engage in polite conversation, feared having to offer commiserations when he endured no real sorrow; he felt more than ever now his inability to sympathise, his lack of a really true involvement, and he was honest enough with himself, at least on this particular morning, to admit that the recent weeks of solitude had not put this want in him for the first time: they had merely crystallised and given shape to what had always been there.

Yet when he began to meet people he took their proffered hands, and shook his head, and murmured words which remained on his tongue for a long time afterwards like the fetid taste of some long unsought despair. He even allowed himself to be brought into the room where Father Manton's body was laid, the face yellow and unlined and cast in a waxlike mould of utter stillness; and nothing touched him in the silence of that morgue-like room either, except the desire to leave as quickly as possibly.

Afterwards he went down to the lake and sat in what remained of a beached canoe and looked out over the water. A little way from him a number of small boys threw stones at the body of a dead Federal soldier which came and went with the motion of the waves, and the ever-present egrets picked their dainty way about in the tall grass to his left. The fishermen were out again, flinging their nets like canopies of cobwebs over the water, and their shouts echoed and re-echoed over the placid surface of the lake as they made a catch, or narrowly missed one. Soon it began to rain, random drops which broke the still water into concatenations of overlapping ripples, and a small wind clicked through the reeds which grew in the shallows, and gently rocked the boats of the fishermen.

When the rain became heavier Painter got up and made his way back through the town. An old man walked beside him for part of the way and held a battered umbrella over his head, but he turned away apologetically outside the priest's house and went in presumably to pay his last respects. Painter walked on, up the hill and around by the deserted hospital, while the rain increased in volume and the pathway became a morass of mud under his feet. He had almost got to his house when he looked up and saw the car standing in the driveway. It was an ancient red Volkswagen, with the right front wing missing, and it was badly in need of a coat of paint, and for a moment Painter thought that perhaps Igor was not really dead after all and had come again to visit him as he had so often done in the past.

He walked up the pathway and stood on the verandah. Ben Nzekwe was sitting in the living room wearing a grey army uniform. He looked healthy and well-fed, and his beard lay full and bushy over the collar of his shirt like a badge of honour. When he saw Painter he stood up and put out his hand as if inviting him in, then he said, "I couldn't

191

find you in the town. I've come to take you to Uli. Colonel Ozartu feels the time has come for you to leave."

Painter went into the room and sat down in his wet clothes in the only other chair. He put his feet out in front of him and looked at the red mud stains on his shoes and on the bottoms of his trouser legs. He said, "So the time has come for me to leave."

"Yes, you have been here long enough. One might even say that you have outstayed your welcome."

"Are you blaming me for something, Ben?" Painter said. Suddenly he grinned. "I see you've finally joined the army," he went on. "Your uniform sits well on you. Could you not have found one for me?"

Nzekwe shrugged. "It means very little," he said. "I make a very poor soldier. I take part in no battles. It is only when the fighting stops that I arrive. I am too valuable to risk being shot at – at least that is what I am told."

"And you believe it?"

"Why not? It gives one a sense of importance, a sense of one's proper place in the order of things. It is comforting to know that people are willing to die on one's behalf. I, and others like me, will survive because we are the planners and the organisers – we will shape and stabilise the new nation when it emerges from the present chaos. We are the leaders."

"Jesus Christ," Painter said. He looked closely at Nzekwe. "Are you beginning to believe your own propaganda?"

"No, I'm merely playing a part like all the others. Have you learned nothing in the months since I have last seen you? There is no point in being an outsider – life passes one by."

Painter leaned forward in his chair. His face was blue with cold and his eyes gleamed as if he had fever. He pointed his finger at Nzekwe – "I remember once telling someone that even the act of giving in requires courage," he said. "Perhaps it's a courage of despair."

192

Nzekwe shuffled his feet impatiently and got up. He stood with his back to the door, and the grey light pressing all around him seemed to blur his outline and to strip away some of the authority from his military uniform and bearing. "You speak your words as if you had rehearsed them," he said to Painter, with something akin to anger in his voice. "They are empty, as empty as your actions. You have no depth. There are no small dark places in your mind, no recesses of sunlight and shade, no resources that you can call upon ..." He paused, then he went on, "I was sent to give you a message. You will be ready at six o'clock in the morning, and an army lorry will take you to Uli. I can do no more than deliver the message. Any other conversation is of no importance. You are nothing more than an acquaintance to me, someone that I knew a long time ago and who made no impression on me then either. I will see you in the morning."

He turned away and went out into the rain. After a moment Painter heard the sudden roar of the Volkswagen's engine, then the swish of its tyres in the gravel of the drive, and then silence. When all sound had faded he got up and ran out onto the verandah, as if it was only then he realised that Nzekwe had really gone. The sudden movement brought drops of sweat to his brow, and his chest heaved with the unaccustomed exertion. He stepped off the verandah and let the curtain of mist brush against his face, and as he felt its coolness he imagined it sweeping soddenly away across the hill, and down into the town where it would also embrace the priest's house in which Father Manton's body lay, cold and stiff and slowly turning into dust. He began to shiver violently.

13

Darkness fell quickly from the lowering clouds and blotted out the objects in the room, and still Painter sat silently and did nothing. His mind was overflowing, yet, when he tried to think, his thoughts fell apart like ash from a mosquito coil. Once he caught himself giggling helplessly, but the reason for his doing so eluded him, and he began to wonder if he were going mad. He swung his hands between his legs and paid no attention to the sticky dampness of his clothes, or the uncontrollable shivering which gripped him from time to time. He felt that he had come to an ending of sorts, as if he had been watching the unreeling of some film and was now awaiting the switching on of the lights and the self-conscious coughs and twitchings of the audience who had been watching with him. He could only think of little things: vague gestures and half-formulated scraps of conversations, voices and faces which blurred into greyness and then reformed themselves into other voices and other faces when he tried to concentrate on them. There was no continuity, no linking up of incidents or feelings, no highs or lows; his mind seemed to be moving with a sickening placidity towards the edge of an abyss, and yet there was nothing that he wished to do about it. Not for the first time he sensed a depth of inadequacy in himself, an inadequacy which hitherto had manifested itself only as a restlessness in the face of the kind of set situations and ordinary everyday relationships which other people seemed to glide through unconcernedly. He had never deliberately avoided decisions, he had merely allowed them to float away from him like debris sailing aimlessly down a stream. How many times had he settled, not for second best, but for third or fourth best, and then persuaded himself afterwards that he had had no choice in the matter? How many people had he been untrue to by pretending that he enjoyed their company, and how many other people had he alienated from him because he feared their love? He had thought that over the years he had built up a well of self-sufficiency, but now he realised that this self-sufficiency was composed of an ethical nihilism supported on a tide of secondhand mannerisms and soiled dreams. There was nothing really that he cared about, no religious concept, no political philosophy, no one thing that he could passionately embrace and become a part of; and yet the desire for such a thing tormented the edges of his conscious mind like the sighing of a mnemonic wind. In the end perhaps that is all he would be left with: a sense of failure without ever having really tried, and a memory only of something that he had once aspired to and now no longer recognised. He sighed and shifted restlessly in his chair. Perhaps, he thought, I have already arrived at that point, have passed it by, and have entered a terrain of mind where silence reigns, instead of hope.

Suddenly he raised his head and stared about him at the darkness. Had he heard his name being called? Or had it merely been wish fulfilment on his part – another little ruse to interrupt his flow of half-felt reverie, to give himself once again the urge to carry on? He decided not to make any movement whatsoever, but immediately, without even consciously changing his mind, he began to fumble about for the stub of candle which he had left beside the matches on the table near him. When he had it lit he got up and went to the door. The night was very black and the air had a moist smell, but the rain had stopped falling. At first he could see nothing unusual, but then in the corner where the low wall of the verandah joined the house he caught a sudden movement. He raised the candle above his head, and the small circle of light widened and feebly fell across a figure sitting crouched against the wall.

For a moment Painter could distinguish no details, and even when the head was raised and he could see the face he still found it difficult to believe that it was Captain Basanji that he was looking at. He was wearing only a pair of ragged shorts, and a frayed rope tied his wrists at about knee level to his ankles.

Painter went closer, holding the candle out in front of him like a weapon. He bent slightly, and when he could see the Captain's face clearly he felt the strength go out of his legs, and he slid down with his back against the wall until he was also sitting in a crouched position, facing the other man. A sharp instrument, probably a six-inch nail, had been driven down through the top of the Captain's head, and the point of it protruded out of his right eyebrow as an icy glitter in the candlelight. The motion of blinking had caused the nail to wear a jagged red wound in his eyelid and the whole right-hand side of his face was streaked with dried blood like grave-clay.

When he saw Painter looking at him the Captain turned his face away and said hoarsely, "Put out the light. I do not wish you to see me like this," but when Painter had extinguished the candle and the darkness had settled in around the two of them again, he could still see the Captain's face clearly in his mind's eye. "I do not want your pity," the other man went on. "I have come to ask a favour of you. I want you to kill me."

For a moment Painter did not answer him. He felt the roughness of the wall against his back, and the small irritation where the base of his spine met the stone floor; he could hear himself breathing audibly through his mouth

196

and could sense the heat between his thumb and index finger from the wick of the candle. Quite suddenly these tiny sensations seemed to mean a lot to him, seemed to take on a definitive clarity which was more important to him at that moment than anything else. All at once the need to analyse these minutiae came to be of the most pressing urgency; he felt that they held within them, like the play of light in a jewel, the secret of some hidden mystery. It took a conscious effort on his part to drag his mind back and to concentrate on the man in front of him, and even when he did, he could still feel other small perceptions disturbing his concentration like drops of water dripping from a tap. It was as if on the point of his breaking through to a whole new depth of awareness he had become distracted by the voice and troubles of an unwanted companion, and yet these same distractions of themselves formed an integral part of the variant framework which produced the revelation. Something nuzzled at his mind, at the greyest edge of his consciousness, something which was too precious to be fully realised, or too crystalline in its utter perfection to be ever really attainable, and yet something, as he knew with a despairing certainty, that had been born in the depth of his vision by the turning away of his mind from other more important things. Had he deviated once too often, he wondered, from the chance of becoming involved? ... and was he now being tantalised by the dying fall of what he might have grasped if he had been capable of a different sort of compromise? He thought, If I could have one more chance; but the words fell through his mind like the echo of a mocking laugh, and he said aloud to the Captain, or perhaps merely to the darkness, "I can do nothing. Like you, I have lost. I'm as mutilated as you are."

"It's not the pain, you understand," the Captain said, and his voice had become stronger. "I can stand that. It would not have mattered how they had tortured me if I had died. It's the indignity of being seen like this, of being spat upon. They are out there now in the darkness watching me. They guard me as carefully as they would a child. They say I killed the priest."

"Once I had the ability to view myself objectively," Painter said. "It was almost as if I were two people. I could adopt one course of action, while in my mind I took a different route. I suppose it was a type of duality born of my belief in my freedom to choose. Yet there were many warnings, like signposts along the way. I never found it easy to weep."

"I had nothing to do with his death," the Captain continued, as if he had merely been waiting for Painter to cease speaking. "I was trapped, just like he was. A person should suffer for what he has done, not for what he might have done. Retribution should be meted out while guilt is still fresh, while the inevitability of punishment is still a conscious fear. Perhaps if I had killed him I would have been allowed to die quickly."

There was movement in the darkness, dim shapes which approached the house and then fell back silently into the enveloping night. Painter saw nothing, but the Captain cried out and tried to hunch himself further into his corner. A star or two winked in the sky, around the shoulders of the threatening clouds, and the smell of the earth was moist and sodden like the odour from a swamp.

"I never missed people," Painter said. "I would think about them, but always in relation to something that they had said or done to me. I never missed them for themselves. I sometimes delighted in letting people see that I did not need them."

Captain Basanji made a small whistling sound as he drew in his breath between his teeth. He said, "They are all around ... watching me ... wondering what I am doing. I'm sure if I asked for food they would give it to me. They blame

198

me for everything – the war, the hunger, the suffering – it is too much. My death should be sufficient. You saw me kill the boy; take my life in return for his."

"It's strange," Painter said, his voice flat and empty, "but when one feels that one has been stripped of the final layer of pretence there is always a further safeguard. It is like a graceful ritualistic dance, with people continually reaching out to one another, but never actually touching. Can the instinct for self-preservation be so strong? Can it bind up wounds before they even occur?"

Again the Captain made a sound of pain, and his bare feet scrabbled on the ground, making a dry rasping noise like paper being torn. "I hear you speaking," he said, "but your words have no meaning for me. Can you not do what I ask? It would only require one blow to end my agony. Otherwise I could live for a day ... a week. They would not punish you for my death. You can say that it was an accident, that in the darkness you became frightened and struck out blindly. It is not correct that I should have to carry the guilt of all."

The people had moved in closer, some of them standing beside the low wall of the verandah and blocking out the light of the stars. They made no sound, they merely stood silently in the darkness like so many shadows, and one was indistinguishable from another. The Captain cowered away from them, but Painter went on obliviously: "There was a time when I could brainwash myself into believing that I was learning from everything that I did and said. I could listen to the puny hopes and fears of the children that I taught, and it was like revisiting some familiar and slightly soiled landscape that I had once lived in myself. I thought I was being true to them by telling them that understanding was the only real basis for enlightenment – I was giving them ashes. There is no understanding, no comprehension; there is only a small hard core of emptiness surrounded by

199

a legion of voices speaking words that mean nothing. Experience is not the fabric against which man can measure the scope of his achievement; there is no happiness to be found there, no laughter, no contentment."

Painter stopped speaking and put his hands around his knees, then he lowered his head and closed his eyes. Hands reached out of the darkness and lifted the Captain and bore him away, and the night became as still and quiet as silence itself.

Part Three

GOLGOTHA

1

In the grey dawn light the garden behind the house did indeed resemble a cemetery. The sticks that had once supported kassava stalks leaned sideways like broken crosses, and the cement blocks which were scattered about might have been fallen headstones. The click of the spades, and the slushing sound of the wet earth as it fell from them, added the necessary cadence to the voices of the mourners, and the crowing of a cock from somewhere in the town was like the exhumation of a darker and more primeval sorrow. The coffin, a rough unplaned wooded box, was bare of ornaments: there were no flowers, no wreaths of sickly lilies – there was only the red mud and the rain-slick foliage of the stunted trees and the grainy canescence of the early morning light.

Ben Nzekwe shifted his feet and watched the gravediggers climb out of the hole they had dug. He stepped aside as the coffin was lifted, and then bowed his head as the rough box was lowered into the grave. One or two of the women began to wail, high and jerky and off-key, and Nzekwe turned his face away irritably from the sound. He thought, It is a bad omen, one should not begin a journey by attending a burial. He tried to remember the face of the priest, but all he could conjure up was a composite of many faces; he had always had difficulty in remembering the features of whitemen – they seemed so alike somehow. He felt a vague sense of shame: the priest had once heard his confession, and now he could not carry the remembrance of the man's face about in his mind for even a short time after his death.

The clay began to thud onto the coffin, making ugly sounds which reverberated through the stillness of the morning air like the dull slaps of exploding mortar shells. The sun had finally managed to push its watery way above the horizon, but the spumescent rolls of cloud drained away its heat and its light, and left it like a reflection seen in a smoke-grimed mirror. Some of the village people lingered on, as if they were unwilling to get back to the business of putting their homes, and their lives, in order once again. Yesterday, and for many days, there had been no point in placing new thatch on a roof, in digging the fields, in performing the ordinary everyday tasks that helped to consolidate the future; there was no future, there was only a long succession of dreary days and nights that were all the same, and which became frozen in a sense of present time that eroded expectation as insidiously as water seeping into sand. They have become used to captivity, Nzekwe thought. He looked at their faces as they stared at the slow filling of the grave, and their eyes were all alike – dull, spiritless ... remote, and he realised that boredom was one of the greatest burdens that the majority of people who became caught up in wars had to bear; so many of the props which kept tedium at bay were removed: the need to be doing something, to be active: the need to feel the pulse beat of time passing, the sudden stab of ... what, gratefulness? ... one experiences upon glancing at a clock and seeing that an hour has passed without one being conscious of its passing. He could imagine what it must have been like for them; perhaps after a time it seemed as if everything had become suspended in a stream of uneventfulness, a static steam in which movement was only an illusion, and where brutality and suffering, and even death itself, were no more than rocks which only surfaced when one drifted close to them.

204

Finally they began to drift away, and as the last of them were swallowed up by the morning mist, Nzekwe stepped forward until he was standing beside the grave. Only himself, Colonel Ozartu and Painter remained, and the morning had now succeeded in pushing the night aside and it was full light.

The Colonel coughed and then spat noisily into the churned-up mud. "It was a poor funeral," he said. He glanced at Painter. "Perhaps someone should have prayed aloud. One of the psalms might have been appropriate."

Painter said nothing, and Nzekwe murmured softly, "It does not matter. Our prayers would be of very little use to him. He had already made his peace with Chukwu."

The Colonel shrugged. "It is the thing to do," he said. "The people would have preferred it."

"Are you always so considerate about the people, Colonel?" Painter suddenly said. He raised his head and looked at the two Africans across the grave from him. His face was as grey as the morning, and a vein pulsed visibly in his forehead just below the hairline. "Why don't you tell them that you are not sure if the Federals did kill Father Manton? Why do you allow them to torture Captain Basanji for something that he may not have been guilty of?"

"I do not know what you mean."

"The Captain visited me last night. He told me that he was innocent of the priest's death."

"But of course he would tell you that. Did he not come to beg some favour of you?"

"He wanted me to kill him."

"Perhaps others in the past have put the same request to him. One has to suffer for one's sins."

"You are changing the subject, Colonel," Painter said. "Last night he was suffering for something that he did not do. At least that is what he told me."

The Colonel spread his hands. "I would have preferred

it if he had been taken as a prisoner of war," he said. "Unfortunately, he was seized by the people before I arrived. I could not demand him back. They have endured enough," he added enigmatically, as if his taking their prisoner from them would have proved to have been the final indignity.

"But they've treated him like a common thiefman," Painter protested.

"And what should he have expected?" The Colonel looked from Painter to Nzekwe. "Was he disappointed that they did not devise some rarer torture for him? Was a nail through his head not exquisite enough? Did he desire something more noble?"

"He saw no nobility in life," Painter said mildly, as if he were beginning to back away from the argument.

"Then why should he look for it in death? It has always been the custom to drive nails through a thiefman's head and to set him free in the bush. Sometimes a man can live for as long as a week. It is a test of a kind also."

"It is like pulling wings off flies."

"Then you think that Captain Basanji deserves no punishment?"

"He deserves to be punished humanely and justly, and not in such a barbaric manner."

The Colonel laughed. He spat again, this time absentmindedly onto the priest's grave. He said, "Our argument is academic. What has happened is in the past. We cannot change it now. The man will soon die, let him have his private agony."

The clouds had rolled away from the face of the sun, and its rays were beginning to suck up the moisture from the earth. The clay in the garden had begun to dry, and the muddy footprints, which had been filled with water, were becoming clearly outlined. Nzekwe was the first to turn away, and as the other two followed him, the Colonel said to Painter, "Why did you not do what he asked you?"

"What he asked me?"

"Yes, the Captain. Why did you not kill him, as he asked?"

"I don't know." Painter looked at Nzekwe, who had waited for them to catch up with him. "I've never killed anyone. I don't know if I could."

"It is quite easy," the Colonel said.

"In anger, possibly. But cold-bloodedly ... ?"

"Could you not have killed him out of pity? Is pity not a more powerful motive than anger?"

"Pity is soft," Nzekwe suddenly said, before Painter could reply. "It diffuses action, rather than focusing it. The only reason to kill is for gain, even if it merely means a few yards of stony ground in the midst of a battle." He paused and stared almost balefully at Painter, then he said, "Captain Basanji was probably telling the truth when he said that he was not responsible for the priest's death. Father Manton was used as a decoy. His companions had been told that if the situation warranted it, they were to kill him and blame it on the Federals. Colonel Ozartu needed the townspeople's anger to help him in taking the town."

The Colonel made a sound which might have been annoyance, but Painter ignored him and said to Nzekwe, "You knew it would happen like that?"

"I know it now."

"Then surely you are not attempting to justify it."

"Justify!" Nzekwe made an angry chopping motion with his right hand. "Do not talk to me about justifying. I have been angry for most of my life. An angry man cannot justify anything."

"Neither does he rationalise everything he does. I have never seen much evidence of your anger."

Nzekwe shrugged and turned away. "I keep it well hidden," he said over his shoulder. "In that way I can draw strength from it."

207

They entered the house, where the coolness of the stone walls and floor contrasted sharply with the heat outside. Painter stared about him at the stark furnishings and the green painted walls. "The last time I was here Father Manton sat in that chair," he said, pointing at a straight backed chair which was drawn up to the wooden table. "He was talking about greengages. His cook had bought a tin of fruit, and the label had fallen off so that neither of them knew what the fruit was. Father Manton was convinced that the tin contained greengages, and he asked me if I knew what they looked like."

"Now it is you who are changing the subject," Colonel Ozartu said. "You were inquiring about the Captain's responsibility in this matter of ..."

"Not responsibility," Painter said, "guilt."

"Is there a difference?" The Colonel smiled and indicated Nzekwe with a nod of his head. "When you were given an answer to your original question you acted as if you had not heard. I expected an outburst of anger, or at least some show of emotion."

"I don't think Mr Painter likes carrying anything through to a conclusion," Nzekwe said mockingly. "He prefers to keep a little something for the future."

"Don't speak for me," Painter said. "I don't want to know anything about it. It's none of my business anymore?"

"When was is part of your business?"

Colonel Ozartu's question was put mildly, but Painter flushed none the less. He said defensively, "I made it part of my business by being involved in it. I ..."

"You never got involved in anything," Nzekwe said. "You merely stayed."

"But don't you see," Painter said, "that was my involvement." As Nzekwe began to shake his head, Painter went on hurriedly – "You and I are alike: we do not make decisions about taking a course of action – it

208

has to be forced on us. We see too many alternatives."

"Cowardice can often find a safe haven among alternatives."

"Are you speaking of moral or physical cowardice?"

"I find little distinction between them, or between moral and physical courage. Cowardice, or courage for that matter, is relative; there are no irrevocable acts where man is concerned. It is only in natural events that such has any meaning: in the tides of the sea, the coming of the seasons of the year, the inevitability of decay and renewal. There are no extremes, there are only little deaths."

"Then how many little deaths, how many humiliations and sorrows does it take before one learns to accept them and to cease fighting?"

"A lifetime of them."

"And what constitutes a lifetime? Is suicide not an irrevocable act?"

"Not at all, unless one believes that there is no life after death. If that is the case then perhaps the act of suicide has some meaning."

Colonel Ozartu gave a snort of impatience, but neither of the other two looked at him. Yet they did not seem to be actively communicating with one another – rather they appeared like men who were trying to find some polite means of ending an argument which had become distasteful to them.

"But death itself is inevitable," Painter finally said resignedly. "Is there to be no fulfilment?"

"Yes," Nzekwe said ambiguously. He turned his back and gazed out through the window at the cloud-reflected morning light. "It is like your shadow going before you," he said over his shoulder. "Death is the time when the shadow will rise up to meet you, and you will step through it, only to find on the other side that nothing has changed, except that your shadow is now behind you. That will be the only difference."

Suddenly Colonel Ozartu walked to the door, as if he at least had come to some decision. As he opened it, he turned and looked back at Painter over his shoulder. "You see," he said, his voice full of derision, "life is an infinite progression of small and inconsequential events leading nowhere. Why then quibble about your own tiny share in it? Go back to the country where you belong, and look for your destiny there. There is nothing further for you here."

As the door closed Painter shut his eyes tightly, and his mouth clenched into a grimace of pain. "Is there nothing left between us, Ben?" he asked. "Have we drifted so far apart?"

Nzekwe turned to look at him. "There was never anything between us," he said. "You merely imagined that I embodied a strength which you lack. In your relationships with people you will always demand, you will never give. You don't know how to give."

"But I want to give. I want to be part of other people's lives. I want to find a home somewhere ..." Painter beat his forehead with his fist like someone punishing himself for an indiscretion. "I want to reach out to something that I know is there, something that has a meaning. I want to travel a road that is going somewhere and doesn't just end in a meandering of little byways. It doesn't have to be a major highway, a bush road would do. Providing that a destination can be arrived at ..."

His voice died away as a sound came from Nzekwe, a harsh, dry choking sound, and Painter could only stop and gape as he saw that the other man was laughing. "I feel that I should applaud," Nzekwe said, when he had got his breath back. "And I would, if this were not a repeat performance which I have heard once too often. I think you have really reached a point of no return. You've gone beyond absurdity into madness. Reality has escaped you. You should have settled for life as it was, and gone and lived it. You are a

Hamlet without emotions, a lover without balls; and I was correct when I said that you are a parasite, you've been living in my mind, and in other people's, for too long. In former times, perhaps, you would have had your tongue cut out; you belong to silence and despair, and you epitomise for me the kind of etiolated thought and culture that the whiteman has brought to my country. Go! Take yourself and your kind out of Nigeria, out of Africa. We are young and strong, but more important, we are alive. Leave us to find our own destinies. We cannot be moulded, we can only be destroyed."

By the time that he had finished Nzekwe was shouting, and for a moment or two after he had ceased speaking his words seemed to hang echoingly in the silence of the room. Painter opened his mouth, but then he closed it again and shrugged his shoulders sullenly. He drew back one of the chairs from the table and sat on it, and he put his hands on the rough wooden surface of the table and began slowly to clench and unclench them. There was a small bell beside his right hand, with a handle shaped in the form of a cross, and he picked this up and aimlessly shook it. It tinkled delicately with a sound like glass beads knocking together. He kept shaking it until Nzekwe suddenly came across to him and snatched it out of his hand. "We must go," Nzekwe said. "Our transport should be ready by now. I shall go with you to Uli. I wish to see you actually board the plane, for I want to be certain that you have really left."

Painter stood up slowly and gazed around the room. Then he looked at Nzekwe. "May I have the bell?" he asked. "I have nothing else to take with me."

"No," Nzekwe said. "You came with nothing, it is right that you should go the same way. It is not the time for the ringing of bells," he added, and he tore the small lead clapper out of its silver hood and threw it on the floor.

211

2

The transport that was waiting to take them to Uli was the same lorry that Father Manton had made his last journey in. Painter and Nzekwe sat in the back on hard wooden benches, in an ordure of stock fish and diesel oil, and their uncomfortable silence was like a physical barrier between them. As they drew away from the house Painter looked back through the open rear end of the truck. Colonel Ozartu was standing at one of the downstairs windows, gazing after them, but he made no gesture of farewell, and before the lorry had turned out through the gateway he had already walked away out of view.

They trundled slowly through the town, past the burnt-out shell of the Welfare Hotel and Igor's damaged, although still imposing, house, and then the lorry was wheezily beginning the ascent of Ogundizzy Hill. In spite of himself Painter looked back, back at the lake and at the school buildings away to his right, but he felt no particular sorrow or gladness in the realisation that he was probably leaving them for the last time. He had put down no roots, had never sought even the trappings of any kind of permanence; the only security he had lived with was the security of an open suitcase and a closed mind. He thought wryly of the dutiful servant in the gospels who buried his talent in the sand, and once again his ability to excuse himself caused him to smile, while at the same time it also made him want to weep.

He returned his gaze to the road, and as the lorry neared the top of the hill it passed a woman walking slowly in the

212

thick mud at the side of the track. They had gone some distance past her before Painter recognised her, but when he did he shouted at the driver to stop and then vaulted over the low tailgate of the lorry and waited in the road for her to catch up with him. He had acted on impulse, but as he watched her come towards him, the girl from the Rivers, he felt a tremor in his mind, like the shade of some half-forgotten promise he had made and then had never kept, and immediately he began to regret his thoughtless action.

The girl was still as he remembered her, but her look of youthful innocence was now slightly blurred, as if in the recent past it had been replaced by something else which had been imperfectly cleaned away. Yet when she saw him standing in front of her she smiled at him and nodded her head, as though she had fully expected to meet him at that place in the road. It still took very little to make her happy.

When she reached him he put out his hand to her, but once again their lack of a common language embarrassed him, and all he could do was smile reassuringly at her. He gestured at the lorry, where it had stopped on the crest of the hill, and when he said, "If you wish, we can carry you a part of your way," she nodded her head as if she had understood his words.

Nzekwe and the driver watched in silence as he helped the girl up into the lorry, and the driver made no attempt to restart the engine. "Tell him to go on," Painter said, and he waved his hand at the man in the front seat to indicate to him that he should continue. The man made no sign that he had heard him, he merely stared fixedly at the girl and remained silent in his seat.

"What's wrong with him?" Painter said. He looked at Nzekwe. "Why does he not go on?"

"He objects to the presence of the girl," Nzekwe said. "As do I."

"But you know her," Painter cried. He caught the girl by

213

the arm and pulled her along the seat until she was facing Nzekwe. "She will be no trouble. We can leave her to wherever she is going."

"How do we know where her way takes her?"

"The road leads only in one direction."

"There are many turnings," Nzekwe said. He turned to the girl and spoke to her in Ibo, but she shook her head uncomprehendingly, and he said in English, "The girl is a fool. She probably does not know herself where she is going."

Painter looked at her, and at the expression in her eyes. He said, "Can we not bring her as far as the tar road? You can see that she is tired. It would be no trouble to us."

"The driver will not take her," Nzekwe said, "and he is the one who decides."

"But why? Why will he not take her?"

"The people have driven her out of the town. She is an outcast, someone who must not be helped in any way. She was Basanji's woman, she lived with him in the town from the time that the Federals occupied it."

"But she's a whore," Painter said in bewilderment. "Sleeping with men is her profession. You have had her, and so have I. She was living with Igor before the Federals came. She will go with whoever pays her. She does not know any better."

Nzekwe shrugged. He turned to the driver and spoke to him in Ibo, and when he had finished speaking the man laughed and shook his head at Painter.

"What did you tell him?" Painter asked, as the engine coughed into life once more and the lorry started forward.

"I told him that the woman is sick, and that she had infected the Captain," Nzekwe said. "I also suggested that if you wished to have her, it would not be right for us to interfere. The man saw the irony of the situation. He does not care very much for whitemen."

214

"Thank you," Painter said almost formally, and for a moment it appeared as though he were going to offer Nzekwe his hand, like someone thanking a stranger for some small service he had rendered.

The lorry dropped over the rise of the hill and gathered speed, and the driver forced the ancient vehicle along the rain-eroded road as if he were in a race. Dirty-brown rainwater shot up from the ruts and spattered against the windscreen, and the rusty wipers did no more than drag a slime of mud backwards and forwards across the glass. Painter lay back against the canvas covering, but the jolting of the lorry made sleep an impossibility and after a time he sat up straighter and watched the road unwind behind them like line from a fisherman's reel.

They must have travelled about halfway towards the tarred highway when the first mortar shell burst in front of them like a giant hammer blow. There was no warning, no sound of its approach; there was merely a dull thump, and then a larger than usual shower of mud and stones hit the front of the lorry. In the interval of its exploding, and the arrival of the next one, the girl threw herself across the space dividing them and clutched Painter about the knees. He was about to lean down to her when the second shell hit the cab, causing the lorry to rear up as if it had run into a brick wall. A long sliver of metal flew through the air and embedded itself in the wooden stanchion beside Painter's head, and as he instinctively ducked, he fell forward on top of the girl and dragged her with him onto the rough splintered floor.

After its first shuddering halt, the lorry gained momentum again, but now it was travelling in a sideways direction, and it wheeled off the edge of the road and toppled over onto its side in the waist-high bush. The three of them – Ben Nzekwe, Painter and the girl – slid along the floor in one tangled heap, and they ended up wedged under one of the seats.

The noise, which had begun so abruptly, died away in ever decreasing ripples of intensity, and Painter felt that he must have lost consciousness for a moment, for he could not remember exactly when the harsh grinding of metal had ceased and the hiatus of stomach-heaving silence had taken over. He was quite comfortable in the shared proximity of the other human bodies, he felt no particular anxiety or sense of pain; rather, his mind and body seemed confined in a warm sensuousness, a cathartic involution of orgiastic contentment which forbade movement or any ordered train of thought. It was a feeling that he would have wished to have had prolonged, but after a time there crept into the silence a small regulated sound, a light plop, plop, plop, as something dripped on him from above. He opened his eyes and looked up at the hand suspended in the air above him with blood running along the little finger, and as it came into his vision his mood broke and fear bloomed once more in his heart like gall.

Nzekwe was the first to disentangle himself, and after a couple of abortive attempts he managed to pull himself up through a large gaping hole in the side of the lorry. Painter pushed the girl up to him, finding her surprisingly heavy, and then he climbed up himself and jumped down into the mud. For some reason the brightness of the sky took him by surprise, and he staggered drunkenly and had to put his hand against the side of the lorry to steady himself. The girl appeared suddenly in front of him, but she veered away and started to walk across the road, and it was only when Nzekwe called to him from above that he went after her and brought her back.

The lorry was lying on its left side with its rear pointing back at the road, and one of the wheels was still revolving slowly as if the vehicle retained one last flicker of life. There was a pungent odour of petrol and charred wood, and a pall of smoke hung in the air as a smudge against the sky. Painter

216

stood with the girl in the circle of his arm and looked about him: at the glaucous sea of waist-high bush, and the flat mud road, and the heavy purplish clouds on the horizon, but there was no sign of life. The muggy air lay flat and palpable about them like air from the interior of a steambath, and the silence was complete; no birds sang, no insects rustled through the undergrowth, no voices, either friendly or hostile, cried out to them. They might have been alone in a wilderness.

After a moment Nzekwe appeared from around the back of the lorry, favouring his right arm and picking his steps carefully in the slippery bush. For no apparent reason he suddenly went back on his heels, and then sat down abruptly with a surprised look on his face. His arm and hand were streaked with bright blood, and his shirt and trousers were black with moisture showing that this was not the first time that he had fallen.

"You're wounded," Painter said. He began to move towards him, but Nzekwe waved him away. "Look to the driver," he said in a weak voice. "I am only slightly injured."

Painter hesitated, then he began to move slowly towards the front of the lorry. The cab had been flattened back into the body of the vehicle; it was a mangled mass of metal and smashed wood, and the windscreen was starred like a spider's web. Painter climbed up on one of the wheels and looked down through the shattered glass. The driver's face glared crazily out at him, the tongue protruding and the eye sockets full of blood, and through a jagged hole in the crown of his head his skull glistened like wet ivory.

Painter looked away until his stomach had recovered its equilibrium. He closed his yes, and then felt his way down from the lorry, but when his feet touched the ground his mood changed once more. Now a blaze of desperation burned in his mind like acid. All of the fear and hesitation seemed to lift from his heart, and he felt a strength in the

217

very essence of his being which refused to accept any further prevarication or excuse. It was as if the sight of the man in the lorry was the final ghastliness, the last horror. Now it was his turn to act, his turn to redress the balance of his former passive acceptance of all that had gone before. He would save Nzekwe, would bring him to some haven where he would be safe and free from pain, and by so doing he would pay his debt, both to himself and to the country. That is the way it has to be, he promised himself, and he made his way back almost gladly to the others.

The girl clutched at him as he went past her, but he shook her off and squatted down on his heels in front of Nzekwe. He appeared to have lost consciousness, but when Painter touched his injured arm he opened his eyes and stared at him. "Ben, listen to me," Painter said. "We've got to get away from here. Whoever attacked us may be Biafrans, but then again they may not. If they are not and they catch you, they will surely shoot you. We must find a safe place to hide."

"Hide! Hide where?" Nzekwe gestured with his left hand at the flat, open country. "There is no place to hide," he said. "To get to the river we would have to cross the road. We could not avoid being seen."

"There must be a way," Painter said. He stood up carefully and looked about him, but the view was empty and barren of movement. Even the clouds which were closing in about the sky seemed to do so imperceptibly, and the few drops of rain which were beginning to fall feathered through the fading light aimlessly.

Painter sighed and bent down again in front of Nzekwe. "I can't see any sign of movement," he said. "There's a clump of palm trees about fifty yards across the road from us. That's probably where they are, there's no other cover about. I can't understand why they don't come looking for us," he added, but Nzekwe had closed his eyes again and did not answer.

The girl had been making small clucking sounds in her own language, and when Painter began to examine Nzekwe's wound, she came and stood beside him, but she made no attempt to help. Painter lifted the blood-stained arm and tore away the grey shirt. Nzekwe's armpit was a gory red mass, but the bleeding had stopped, and whatever had struck him did not appear to be still in the wound. Painter motioned to the girl to hold the arm in the air. At first she hesitated, but he caught her by the shoulder and forced her to hold the bloody limb aloft. He pulled out the tail of his own shirt, and in attempting to tear part of it off, only succeeded in stripping most of the shirt from his body. He ripped it into narrow strips and bound up the wound. Finally he used one of the sleeves to fashion a rough sling. When he had finished he sat back and surveyed his handiwork. He felt pleased, for it looked quite professional.

Across the road the soldiers had been arguing among themselves, but after a time they had come to some decision and now they were moving cautiously out of the trees, spreading out and crawling on all fours through the scanty cover afforded them by the stunted bush. They were not expert soldiers, and they made a lot of noise: their boots slipped against the wet roots, metal clinked against metal, one of them sneezed in a tiny explosion of sound; if they had been stalking a wild animal it would have run away from them long before.

It was the girl who noticed them first, but she had to make several attempts before she could draw Painter's attention to what she had seen. She was like a small captive bird rushing against the bars of its cage as she dragged at his arm, and she collapsed breathlessly against him when he finally stood up and looked in the direction she was pointing.

At that moment Nzekwe suddenly opened his eyes and cried out, as if he were only beginning to feel the pain of his wound for the first time. Painter dropped down beside him, dragging the girl with him, and his gesture of putting his finger to his lips had the desired effect for when Nzekwe spoke, it was in a whisper. "What is it?" he said. "What do you see?"

"There are people moving out there," Painter said. "I can't see them clearly, but they're coming in our direction."

Nzekwe groaned and leaned back against the lorry. "I'm tired," he said. "Take the girl and go. It will serve no purpose for all of us to remain here."

"No," Painter said. "I'm taking you with me."

"Why should you wish to do that?"

"I want to bring you back, Ben. I want to do that much for you. I owe it to you."

"I see," Nzekwe said. He blinked through the rain at Painter." Don't trust too much to appearance," he said. "I am not as weak as I may seem. It is merely a question of my not wishing to go any further. It is a gamble. I will take my chances with whoever is out there."

"No," Painter said again. He shook his head. "Everyone wants to live a little longer. Tomorrow you will thank me."

"Tomorrow I will curse you, as I curse you now. Leave me to find my own way."

"Oh dear Christ," Painter knelt in the mud and raised his hands like a supplicant, while the rain beat down on him with ever increasing venom. "I must do some one thing," he cried. "You cannot deny me this chance. I have dreamed of freedom, just as you Ibos have dreamed of it. It is my war as much as yours."

"You are welcome to it." Nzekwe covered his eyes with his good arm. "This war is only a link in a chain, a flight away from boredom. The greatest curse I can wish upon you is that you should continue to have the ability to dream. Go away from me. You are a monster. God has truly forsaken you."

Suddenly Painter reached out and caught Nzekwe by the arm. They began to struggle, silently and savagely, and he had almost succeeded in wrestling the other man to his feet when he suddenly cried out and pointed over Painter's shoulder. "The girl," he gasped. "What is she doing?"

Painter looked behind him and saw the girl from the Rivers walking away from them. She was moving slowly but purposely towards the road, a small upright figure in her wraparound, and the hard, desultory rain fell on and about her and made no sound. "Go after her," Nzekwe said into Painter's ear. "She does not know what she is doing. Those soldiers will not pay her money for her services. They will use her like an animal."

Painter released Nzekwe and moved after the girl. He caught up with her and pulled her down, but when he took his hands off her she stood up again and continued on her way. He caught her for the second time and she struggled for a moment, and as her wrap opened he saw with surprise that she was heavily pregnant. They paused in the middle of the wet bush like a pair of dancers frozen in an awkward embrace, and then the girl raised her arm and caressed Painter's face. She took his hand and pressed it to the swell of her stomach, and there was a resigned finality about the movement which caused Painter to make no further protest when she once more turned and walked in the direction of the road. She passed out of his life as quietly as she had entered it, and it was only when he saw her cross the road that he realised that he did not even know her name.

He crouched down and retraced his steps to the lorry, to where Nzekwe was slowly struggling to his feet. "What have you done?" he cried, as he managed to stand up. "Why did you not bring her back?"

"Never mind," Painter answered him. "It was of her own choosing. She will delay them for a little time. It will be enough."

221

He put out his hand to Nzekwe, but he pushed him away. "Leave me," he groaned. "I cannot bear to look at you."

"But you've got to come away," Painter said desperately. "The girl has sacrificed herself for you ..."

"Not for me." Nzekwe shook his head. The mud in his hair and beard made him look like a very old man, and his face had the greyish colour of weathered slate. "She did it for you. She is another of your victims."

"She asked nothing of me," Painter said. "She was there when I needed her, yet I never thought about her. Now I will have to live with her to the end of my days."

Nzekwe made no reply. All of his strength seemed to have left him and he sagged forward and would have fallen if Painter had not caught him. He dragged him down into the undergrowth beside him and began to crawl along by the side of the lorry. When he was clear of its protective shield he hoisted Nzekwe up onto his back, and running in a stooped position he made his way as fast as he could through the bush in a direction parallel to the road. Once he imagined he heard the girl scream, but it could have been the sighing of the wind.

After a time he stopped to rest and he raised his head and looked back cautiously, but he could see no sign of anyone pursuing them. It could only have been early afternoon, but the lowering sky blotted out the light, and the resultant murkiness cast a gloom over the land.

He continued on, and at a bend in the road, they crossed over to the other side. Painter began to move faster, threshing his way violently through the clinging bush and not bothering about any effort at concealment. Something inside him drove him on; he felt a fierce exhilaration in their wild flight, and after a time all that mattered to him was the reckless momentum of his charge through the bush.

It was only when Nzekwe began to scream that Painter realised that he was dragging him by his injured arm. He

222

stopped, half bent over, and looked down at the man beneath him. The rain had begun again, hard driving rain out of a storm darkened sky, and Nzekwe was plastered with grey mud which clung to him like an extra layer of skin. He was fully conscious and his eyes burned feverishly out of his clown's mask of clay – they stared malevolently at Painter with an intensity of passion which belied the seeming physical weakness of the rest of him. His wound had broken open again and bright crimson blood was seeping through the mud-stained bandages.

"I don't know where we are," Painter said. Now that the abruptness of their flight had ceased he suddenly felt a deep exhaustion as if the energy which had sustained him so far was now completely dissipated.

Nzekwe struggled up into a sitting position. He coughed and then spat on the ground. "The river is surrounded by mangrove swamps," he said. "Watch for the trees, and you will know that we are near it when you see them."

Painter took off the remainder of his shirt and wiped Nzekwe's face with it, and then his own. "How do you feel, Ben?" he asked. "Will you be able to carry on?"

Nzekwe shrugged. "I am cold," he said. "Especially my feet. I cannot feel them. I have never been so cold before. Even in London when the ice was on the lake ..."

"That's because you have lost some blood. We will soon be back in Ogundizzy, and then you can sleep."

"Sleep." Nzekwe smiled grimly. "It is a long time since I have slept peacefully. I am haunted by dreams. I see myself sinking slowly into a vast sea of shifting sand, silently and without a struggle. It has been a gradual process. One lingers on despite oneself."

"Don't talk like that, Ben." Painter took off Nzekwe's boots and began to rub his feet. "You see," he went on, "it is only your imagination. Your wound is nothing. In a week you will not even know it was there."

223

"It will always be there," Nzekwe said in a weak voice. "It is a wound which had been eroding my will for a long final time. I cannot live in captivity. I feel no pain."

"It is not necessary to feel pain," Painter said. "Shame, frustration, doubt, any one of those is a good substitute. As long as there exists a paucity of answers, then interest will be rekindled. Tomorrow you will ask yourself why you felt like this today."

"Yes, perhaps you are right." Nzekwe looked almost slyly at Painter's bowed head. "We must continue on and get to the river before darkness falls. You must not be disappointed."

Painter raised his head. "What do you mean?" he said. "How will I not be disappointed?"

"You wish to save me, do you not?" There was a note of gaiety in Nzekwe's voice. "Your faith is still intact. In spite of yourself you still believe in a just God. You will gain something, some measure of fulfilment by bringing me back. I would not wish to deny you that."

"You're making fun of me," Painter said. Then he grinned through the mud on his face. "But it's a good sign. Perhaps we can salvage something after all."

Nzekwe made no reply, and after Painter had put his boots back on and relaced them, they continued on. After a time the rain blew itself out, and as evening drew on the sky cleared, and when the sun began to set it did so in a brilliant glaze of serrated light which softened the outline of the countryside and lit up the small pockets of unevaporated rainwater like jewels. They came to the mangrove swamp, and their progress was considerably slowed by the clinging mud. Nzekwe began to have periods of semi-consciousness when he babbled deliriously in a mixture of English and Ibo, and Painter had to stop more and more often in order to rest. It was night by the time they got to the river, a placid, sliding flood under the light of a moon which had appeared as abruptly as if it had been switched on; but they came out near a village and Painter was able to steal a small canoe without being seen. He had difficulty in getting Nzekwe into it, and they were both covered in leeches by the time that he managed to push them out into the middle of the stream.

The canoe drifted silently along with the current, and Painter lay as he had fallen. At first he tried to dislodge the leeches from their tenacious hold in his flesh, but he soon gave up and began to doze. Once he awoke to the echoes of a cry reverberating in his mind, but whether it was Nzekwe or himself who had shouted he did not know. He fell asleep again and dreamed that Anne Siena was with him in the canoe. They were setting out on a picnic, and the girl was wearing a filmy dress which lay about her slender ankles like thistledown. They were both talking and laughing, as the dappled water slid slowly past and disappeared in a misty haze of sunlight, and the large white bird which had alighted on the prow of the canoe opened and closed its beak as if it were yawning. The girl continued to laugh as Painter began to tell her how much he loved her, and as her laughter became louder it seemed to stir the surface of the water so that eventually the canoe started rocking from side to side like a cork. The more the canoe started rocking the angrier Painter became, but the girl went on laughing until all he could see was the raw red wound of her mouth and the wetness of a tongue which looked as if it were preparing to reach out and drag him into the shiny moist cavern behind it. The sun disappeared and a wind began to blow, and as the darkness fell about them Painter awoke full of terror to find himself scrabbling furiously backwards along the tarred bottom of the canoe.

After that he slept and woke a number of times. Once or twice he tried to talk to his companion, but he also slept, or pretended to, and made no answer. The night drifted slowly by, as quietly as the river, and it was just before dawn when the early morning fishermen found them and brought them to the shore of Ogundizzy Lake. Painter awoke for the time as the canoe was beached on the rough gravelly sand, and as he blinked in the light of the flickering torches he saw Ben Nzekwe being lifted out and placed gently at his feet. He looked so still and peaceful that Painter began to get afraid and he tore at the arms which sought to restrain him and caught Nzekwe in his arms.

"We're safe, Ben," he cried, as he cradled the other man's head against his chest. "Our journey is over."

There was no reply, and after a moment one of the fishermen leaned down and spoke into Painter's face. "This man go die'o," he said calmly. "He no be there anymore."

"No," Painter said. He shook the inert body in his arms. "He's not dead, he's only sleeping. It's been a long time since he has slept," he added, and he smiled vacantly at the circle of faces about him.

The man who had spoken shook his grizzled head. "He be wounded too much," he said. "Look at how he bleeds." He tried to disengage Painter's arms, but he pulled away and buried his face against Nzekwe's. He began to rock backwards and forwards, and he made an odd keening sound in his throat. The fisherman spread his hands and shook his shoulders expressively. "That man no go help dying," he said to his companions. "How could he live with such a wound?"

"Yes, he could," Painter said from where he was sitting on the ground. "The wound was nothing. He died deliberately, to spite me. He turned his face away from me a long time ago."

The fishermen looked expressionlessly at one another behind Painter's back. One of them bent down and stuck his torch in the sand, where it burned unevenly with a pale blue flame. They began to walk away, but before the last of them had gone Painter spoke once more. "Oh Ben," he said, echoing Nzekwe's own words, "now surely God has forsaken us both."

*

In the second week of January, 1970, the war in Nigeria came to a close. It ended quietly, as the tired tones of a tired voice made a brief announcement over a mobile radio transmitter, but the people, as always, knew beforehand, and even before the flood of anti-climatic news bulletins began to clog the airwaves they were surging aimlessly in panic-stricken flight just as they had done at the beginning of the war.

So this new diaspora brought things full circle, and the dream which had become a nightmare finally shattered totally and left the "land of proud heroes" a torn and devastated place, a place where ceaseless movement was the norm and where the stink of fear rolled almost visibly like yellow fog across the battered landscape.

In the first flush of victory promises were made and although, in accordance with the African rationalisation of the meaning of the word 'brother', many of these promises were kept, time had already passed many of the children by, and they died as listlessly and as effortlessly as birds frozen by the cold of winter. All of the foreign powers which had helped to prolong the war now sought to take the credit for ending it. Vast piles of the wrong kind of foodstuffs began to arrive and to rot in various stopping-off places, and a convoy of white-painted ambulances instead of armoured cars now rolled across London Bridge on the first stage of their journey to the newly created East Central State in the Federal Republic of Nigeria.

Biafra belonged only to history ...

Epilogue

RESURRECTION

1

Painter came back to Ireland and, after a period of recuperation, took up a teaching position in a north side Dublin school. But the scars of his sojourn in Nigeria remained. For a time he became a taciturn and cantankerous drunk, avoided by colleagues and friends, and merely tolerated by his family. After one particularly bad binge, when he suffered a blackout that lasted the best part of a week, he began to pull himself together and, with the help of a therapist friend, sorted his life out to a certain extent.

In the beginning, after his return, he talked interminably about his experiences in Nigeria, but he soon realised that people were more taken up with their own preoccupations nearer home. With the collapse of the Biafran secession, the country became divided into twelve federal states, with military rule the order of the day. Yet ethnic and religious tensions remained, the threat of violence was ever present, and the whole economy continued to be based on a system of bribery and favouritism that earned for the country the title of one of the most corrupt places in Africa.

The years rolled by and Painter, as he liked to put it himself, enlarged his life with a multitude of trivialities. Now and then he still awoke in the dog hours of the night, awash with the horrors he had seen and experienced in those last awful weeks in Ogundizzy. But time dulled even those abominations, and in his mind's eye they retreated further and further into the shadows.

Then in the 1990s there began a great influx of refugees

231

from Nigeria into Ireland, and Painter, as a form of catharsis, became involved with an agency that helped settle a number of them. And it was at a seminar given by Ken Wiwa, son of the executed writer and activist, Ken Saro-Wiwa, that he met Cletus Okacho, and finally found some little redemption for all the emotive consternation of that troubled time.

It was a rainy evening in Dublin, at the end of a summer that had promised much but in the end had given little. Painter was morose, in the throes of ending a relationship that had burned like sulphur on the head of a matchstick and winked out just as quickly. When the meeting finished, he was introduced to the younger Wiwa, exchanged a few pleasantries and was about to depart when an older, bearded African approached him.

"You are Michael Painter?" he inquired. "You spent some years in Nigeria in the late 1960s?"

Painter admitted that he was, and was then led across to where a younger man was sitting, the white stick by his knee a badge of his blindness. "I am Joseph Obutu," the older man introduced himself, "and this is Cletus Okacho. Cletus has something to tell you, and I will leave him to explain himself. I shall return presently to guide him to his lodgings."

He went away and Painter, after a moment of hesitation, sat down beside Okacho. He appeared to be in his late twenties, heavy-set, a streak of grey like a stripe in his black, curly hair. He was wearing dark glasses, and he now turned these on Painter, causing him to wonder if his companion was partially sighted or totally blind. As though reading his thought, Okacho said, "An accident. A bomb exploded prematurely. You know something of how the Ogoni people are being exploited by the oil companies? They degrade the environment, acid rain eats at tin roofs, the children die in droves from respiratory diseases. Talking and negotiation were useless, so a group of us tried more violent methods."

232

"And did they work?"

"Of course not. We were merely an irritation to the multinational companies. Big business, backed by the more powerful nations. And of course our own crooked politicians. It is the way of the world."

"You sound despondent."

The younger man shrugged. "We do what we can," he said. "But I became merely a hindrance, so they sent me here to lobby your politicians."

"Your English is very good."

"I am from the Rivers people. It is not only the Ibos who knew the value of education. My mother was a very fine woman. She worked so hard to send me to school."

"Oh, yes …?"

Painter shifted in his seat, an itch of foreboding invading his mind. What was he about to be told? he wondered.

"She knew you," Cletus Okacho said, his tone flat and expressionless.

"Your mother?"

"Yes. During the civil war. She often spoke of you."

"I don't quite know …" Painter scratched his head. "It's been such a long time."

"When I came to Ireland, I determined to find this white man that my mother talked about. It was not difficult. You gave a number of interviews to the newspapers at the time. Joseph Obutu looked them up for me."

"Your mother is still alive?"

"No, she is dead now. But she spoke warmly of you. You must have been good to her."

In his mind's eye, Painter remembered the little girl from the Rivers that he had slept with so long ago. It had to be her. The same girl whom he believed had sacrificed herself to the Nigerian soldiers in order to allow him and Ben Nzekwe to escape. Now it seemed that she had not perished after all, but had lived on to give birth to a son.

Hesitantly, he said, "What did she tell you about me?"

"Merely that she knew you, and that you were kind to her."

"Kind?"

Painter was uncomfortable now in this man's presence, but he also felt ashamed. He said, "I try to remember the good things about my stay in Nigeria. The sunrises and sunsets at the beginning and end of the Dry Season, how the skies would flame with colour. The humour of the people. The satisfaction of imparting a little knowledge. And your mother, yes, I remember her too. We had no common language, but when she smiled it brought a tremor to my heart. It was she who was kind to me, not the other way round. And in the end I always believed that she had forfeited her life in order to save mine. I wished then that I'd had the courage to do for her what she had done for me. Now it pleases me to find that she survived and gave birth."

"I never knew my father," Okacho said. "My mother told me he died in the war. Did you know him?"

Thinking of Ben Nzekwe, Painter said, "Yes, I knew him. He was a very fine man. He was my friend. I held him in my arms as he died."

"You know where he's buried?"

An image came to Painter from far back in the past: the greyness of dawn on the shore of Ogundizzy Lake, the pale, flickering blue light of a kerosene torch, the grizzled features of early morning fishermen, and the shallow grave they dug for Ben Nzekwe in the stony soil. What harm would it do now to tell Cletus Okacho that Ben was his father? Among all the men the girl from the Rivers had slept with, he might well have been the one. It would be a fitting epitaph for both of them.

Smiling, Painter put out his hand to Okacho. He said, "It would be a privilege for me to see you home. And we'll talk along the way. May I?"

The other man stood up and grasped his stick. In spite of his infirmity, he stood tall and straight, as he said, "You may see me to my lodgings, but I fear it may be a longer time before you can see me to my home. But the day may come …"

They left the hall and went out the door, someone behind them abruptly switching off all the lights. Yet as they walked down the street, with Okacho's white stick tapping on the pavement, Painter felt a small surge of renewal, as though after a long wait he had been granted a form of completion to a part of his life left suspended in the past.